AF254300

THE MAN IN THE BARN

Digging up Lincoln's Killer

Nate Chura

New Memphis Press

Published by New Memphis Press
www.newmemphispress.com

For information about special discounts for bulk purchases,
please contact New Memphis Press Special Sales at
dear@newmemphispress.com

LIBRARY OF CONGRESS CATALOGING-IN-PUBLICATION DATA
has been applied for.

ISBN: 978-1-63192-620-4
eBook ISBN: 978-1-63192-621-1
Cover and Layout design by Bookbaby Design

For my family

Alas, poor Yorick! I knew him, Horatio; a fellow of infinite jest, of most excellent fancy; he hath borne me on his back a thousand times; and now, how abhorred in my imagination it is!

Hamlet, Act V, Scene I
—William Shakespeare

CONTENTS

AUTHOR'S NOTE

Dear reader,

This novel is a work of fiction. Because it is set against an historical background, its fictional universe includes some characters based on real people, both contemporary and from the past. But the descriptions of people, places and institutions, and the words and actions of the characters, and the events that transpire around them, are wholly the product of my imagination. That imagination has been informed by my extensive research of the historical record and interviews with people knowledgeable about the historic events, but the story is not history; it is fiction and the actions and descriptions of any contemporary figures are purely fictional. The history is intended to serve as the setting for an exciting adventure. I hope that you enjoy the result.

Sincerely,
Nate Chura,
Author, "The Man in the Barn"

MEDIA ALERT

[Sunday, April 26, 20XX, 4:55 AM]

From: <dralpearson@me.com>

To: <info@wikileaks.org>, <edit@nytimes.com>,
<edit@foxnews.com>, <edit@abcnews.com>, <edit@cbsnews.com>,
<edit@nbcnews.com>, <edit@cnn.com>, <edit@msnbcnews.com>,
<edit@washingtonpost.com>, <news@bostonglobe.com>,
<edit@baltimoresun.com>, <news@online.wsj.com>,
<news@newyorker.com>, <news@theatlantic.com>,
<edit@nypost.com>, <edit@dailynews.com>, <news@npr.org>,
<edit@huffingtonpost.com>, <nate54@hotmail.com>

Dear Editor,

I submit the following account for your consideration in response to your recent coverage of the Booth affair, in particular, the results of the DNA test performed on the remains of Edwin and John Wilkes Booth, as announced by the Smithsonian Institution. Please pardon any errors that may appear throughout. Its contents have been hastily composed. In all honesty, I never dreamed I would be doing this. Only out of absolute desperation do I reach out to you now.

Be advised, much of the evidence presented herein runs contrary to many of my previously held beliefs, both as a trained medical physician and a rational human being living for fifty-five years on planet earth, but I leave you to draw your own conclusions. I ask only that you review the information in its entirety and with an open mind, if not for my sake, then for Daniel Boland's.

Up until last spring, Daniel worked as a reporter for the Brooklyn Beacon in New York. He covered the Booth story extensively. He had reason to believe he was a Booth descendant. In addition to the profile match performed between John and Edwin, Daniel submitted a DNA sample of his own to affirm his relation to the brothers. The result of the test had a marked effect on him.

Please know I'm well aware that I am not the ideal person to be presenting this information. The only reason I am probably still alive and well enough to write this now is because the powers that be must deem me such a discreditable witness that no one would believe me.

It's true. I am a disgraced medical doctor. Over the course of twenty years I amassed a small fortune as a Manhattan psychiatrist. I owned a thriving private practice. Then two years ago an extremely chemically unbalanced young man, who shall remain nameless, came into my office with his mother. By now I've looked over his chart a thousand times to try and remember more detail than that, but every time I draw a blank. My notes are completely indecipherable and, at this point, it makes no difference. After he jumped off the Queensboro Bridge two days later his mother came after me and my medical license with all her might.

It's true. I was not fit to perform my job. I am an alcoholic. I let her son slip through my fingers and now, again, Daniel has slipped away, too. I have lied to myself and to others close to me once too often, but I swear on the last shred of dignity I have left, every word contained in this account is true…to the best of my knowledge. I hope by sending it to you Daniel's efforts, at least, will not have been in vain.

At this point, I have done all that I can do. The rest is up to you. I thank you in advance for your time and understanding.

Yours truly,
Dr. Al Pearson
16 Gramercy Park South
New York, NY 10003

THE PLAYERS

I guess you could say my involvement in this ordeal began over two decades ago when a friend of mine convinced me to join The Players, the legendary New York theatre club founded in the late-nineteenth century by renowned Shakespearean actor Edwin Booth, of the once famous Booth theatrical clan. The money was really flowing in for me at that point, and I had always been a fan of the theatre, so I was rather expeditiously admitted to the club as a "Man of the Theatre." Members of this classification are the VIPs of the club. We're the prospective producers for the multitude of theatrical enterprises forever being cooked up in Edwin's old kitchen. We're also very good about buying drinks for the talent.

For years I enjoyed the club in this fashion, as a respectable patron of the arts. I used to drop by after work for a drink or two and enjoy a smoke out on the balcony, which overlooks Gramercy Park. Occasionally I'd trade a few laughs with some of the old has-beens of yesteryear, then I'd go on with my life and day to day responsibilities. After my wife and I separated three years ago, however, my relationship to The Players changed dramatically. It became my sole refuge from a world that was spiraling violently out of control. It contained me. When not at work, I was at the club. I ate, drank, read, slept, lived at The Players. There's no place in the world quite like it.

The instant you enter the front door you feel like you've stepped back in time. It's dark and warm and smells like tobacco and old books, and everywhere you look you see old paintings and other priceless artifacts, like Mark Twain's famous pool stick and General Sherman's old beer mug. But also, and most importantly these days, all the chairs are plush and comfortable. You can recline in them for hours and drink until you can't speak, the way James Cagney and Humphrey Bogart and the rest of the gang used to back in the golden days, which is exactly how I found myself the February afternoon I detail for you now.

I was reclined in my usual spot beside the fire in the grill when I was jolted out of my seat by a violent thunderbolt. The instant I came to I saw a figure grinning at me from across the pool table. It was Daniel Boland. It must have been pouring out, because he had on a raincoat and was leaking on the floor.

"You alright, Doc?" he asked.

"Daniel," I said, alarmed. "What the hell are you doing here at this hour? Shouldn't you be at work?"

"I took the afternoon off," he said.

"And you decided to come here?"

"I was really craving a game of pool."

I knew then and there something was up, but it took a while for Daniel to come out with it.

I first met Daniel roughly half a dozen years ago at some cocktail party or other in the Great Hall. His presence was striking, a cross between a well-mannered diplomat and some ancient general. Julius Caesar, perhaps? Whatever spirit he conjured, the effect was amplified by the whisper that rapidly began swirling around the parlor. Rumor had it Daniel was a distant Booth relative from an estranged branch of the family who had decided to reconcile his roots and join the club. Members were falling all over each other to speak with him. Now, as he bounced out of the men's room, his hair and shoes freshly blow-dried, he had the run of the place.

"Rene," he called out to our bartender, "I'll have what he's drinking."

Sporting a spiffy blazer and neatly pressed slacks, Daniel was completely transformed. He looked like a movie star. The moment he sat down Rene appeared with his drink, which he immediately shot in one gulp.

"I'll have another whenever you get around to it," he said, before Rene could walk away.

"Tough morning at the Beacon?" I asked.

"Always," he said. The Beacon was the last thing Daniel wanted to talk about, and with good reason.

Daniel was very bright. He graduated an All-American from Villanova University. He played first-base for the Wildcats. He always told me he could catch anything, but couldn't throw to save his life. I also understand his hitting wasn't all that impressive either, but none of that mattered. Sports were secondary to Daniel. His true passion was journalism. He loved everything about it. He loved how you get to see things and meet people that most people don't. He loved the rush of a deadline. He loved that every story was an opportunity to learn something new. He also fully subscribed to the notion that fact is usually stranger than fiction. So when he landed the internship at the Beacon, he didn't blink twice. He moved to New York, almost instantly, with his girlfriend Shelly.

In the final analysis, this move may have been Daniel's biggest error. Not moving to New York, but moving to New York with Shelly. He might have been able to weather the Beacon, if he didn't have her success to contend with. He might have been able to make a transition or maybe he would have just packed up and gone home. We'll never know.

I never met Shelly, but I understand she was a smart, ambitious, young woman. She and Daniel were college sweethearts and graduated in the same class. I've also been told she was a stunning beauty, but that was only part of her allure. "Shelly had this incredible aura," Daniel said. "People wanted to be around her. Without even trying, the world always seemed to rotate around her."

Within a month of moving to New York, she landed a job at a prestigious Manhattan marketing firm and within three years was earning three times as much as Daniel, who had been hired as a full-time "reporter" at the Beacon in the same amount of time. I put quotes around the word "reporter" because Daniel spent more of his time at the "bureau" tediously cutting and pasting and rewording legal notices and new business announcements than he did actual reporting. Occasionally, he would turn out some story about the Gowanus Canal or some new citywide trend in parking tickets, but it was certainly a far cry from the exhilarating news he imagined he would be covering when he moved to the city.

Despite it all, Daniel said he kept a positive outlook in those early years. It took him a while to truly discover how life in New York can grind you to the bone. But as day after day passed painfully punching in legal notice after legal notice, the agony of slaving away at the machine gradually began to take its toll on him, especially when he compared all the rewards Shelly was raking in from her job.

I suppose he could have gone to another paper or magazine. He said he looked into that at one point, but discovered he wouldn't have made any more money and would, essentially, be doing the same thing, proofing and banging out an endless stream of words each day about shit he could care less about. The switch wasn't worth the hassle. Then before he knew it, all those options started drying up, as paper after paper and magazine after magazine began to fold. The Beacon miraculously managed to keep printing, which was a strange blessing, and a wicked curse.

So there he was, stuck at the Beacon, while Shelly and all her friends were gaily climbing the corporate ladder. And the more money she began to bring in, the more he began to resent the whole situation. It slowly began to poison their relationship. At first he didn't notice it. He couldn't exactly explain why they weren't getting along anymore, but eventually it all came pouring out. Before long they were fighting about everything, money, independence, what might happen, God forbid, if they ever decided to get married and have kids, and other endless variations on the same theme. Daniel couldn't stand it. He felt like a total failure.

Then one day Shelly came home and told him she had had enough. She was leaving him. And she didn't lie. Within a month, Shelly had completely vanished from his life. It totally devastated him. Now I'm not convinced Daniel's lack of success is what drove her away. It's common for young people to change and drift apart, but that's not how Daniel read it. He ultimately acknowledged the breakup as a painful wakeup call that he needed to be doing more with his life. From that day forward, he vowed he would make something of himself. He may have lost Shelly, but he'd be damned if anyone would ever leave him again because he wasn't good enough. As Daniel shot circles around the pool table that wet February afternoon, he stayed true to that vow.

"I got word from Nate this morning," he said, as he lined up a shot. "The museum is going to allow the testing."

My heart skipped two beats.

My first real conversation with Daniel had been over this same pool table. On that occasion, I asked him if the rumors were true he was related to Booth. I was surprised when he told me he didn't know, in fact he knew very little about his ancestry.

For starters, he said, he had no memory of his father, who was killed in a car accident when he was an infant. Daniel's mother almost never spoke about him. And as for his father's parents, they also died when Daniel was very young. It wasn't until sometime in high school that Daniel's grandmother, on his mother's side, began telling him more about his father. He specifically recalled being startled one day when she told him that his father was really a Booth, even though his last name was Boland. She explained that the Bolands changed their name generations ago to avoid the stigma cast upon it after the Lincoln assassination.

Daniel admitted that, as fascinated as he was by the revelation at the time, the topic was never spoken about again, and he more or less forgot about it. It wasn't until Shelly left him that he fully began to process what his grandmother told him all those years ago, and then the questions flowed. His search for answers is what led him to Edwin. It's what led him to The Players. It's what led him to me.

Now, watching him shoot pool in front of the flickering fire, talking as if no time had passed since our first conversation, Daniel overwhelmed me with a flood of new facts about the Booths. It was as if, in between drinks, he had become a pre-eminent Booth scholar. In reality, he had. When Daniel walked into the club that afternoon, he was well on his way to writing the greatest story about the Booths ever written. Or so he thought.

"What do you mean they're going to allow the testing?" I asked.

"Well it's not a lock just yet," he said, "but Nate called me and told me, just this morning, that Congressman Christopher finally submitted the proposal to the museum a few weeks ago and he just got the unofficial word that they're going to green light it." He took a drink. "Which means now all we have to do is dig up Edwin."

2

EDWIN BOOTH

These days very few people know who Edwin Booth was. He's usually referred to as the brother of the guy who shot Lincoln. But during his lifetime, Edwin was truly one of the most prominent and well respected men in the country. Some theatre historians consider him the father of modern acting.

Unlike his melodramatic contemporaries, Edwin was a naturalistic actor. His performances were more subtle and realistic. There is evidence that he influenced the revolutionary acting techniques of Constantin Stanislavski, the first recognized method actor. But Edwin's talents went far beyond subtle interpretations of Shakespeare. He was also a theatrical visionary who invented Broadway as we know it today. He built the Winter Garden Theatre and became the first actor in history to perform the role of *Hamlet* one hundred nights in a row.

In his day, Edwin Booth was as famous as Mark Twain or Ulysses Grant, who also happened to be his good friends. Certainly neither of these men could have imagined that Edwin's legacy would amount to playing a supporting role in the tragedy created by his less talented brother, John. Of course, everyone still remembers John. He's a household name.

Every grade-school student in the country learns about John Wilkes Booth, the infamous mustachioed assassin. He was a famous actor and Southern sympathizer who killed President Abraham Lincoln in a fit of madness during the last days of the American Civil War. It's an inescapable part of the national curriculum.

The classic story goes that on April 14, 1865, during a performance of "Our American Cousin," John Wilkes Booth crept inside the presidential box on the mezzanine of Ford's Theatre in Washington, D.C. and shot the President in the back of the head with a derringer pistol. He then jumped to the stage and shouted, "Sic semper tyrannis," and raced out of the theater and into the pages of history.

Thanks to books like *Manhunt*, and documentaries like *Killing Lincoln*, and a slew of other titles, students are taught that after Booth miraculously managed to flee the capital on horseback with a broken leg, a highly complex operation was launched to catch him. Hiding out in the swamps and marshlands of Maryland and Virginia, the most notorious killer in the nation's history escaped capture for twelve days after Lincoln was pronounced dead.

Finally, on April 26th, Union forces caught up with the assassin at Richard Garrett's farm near Port Royal, Virginia. The Sixteenth New York Cavalry and a hand full of special agents from the War Department surrounded Garrett's barn, where Booth and his accomplice David E. Herold were hiding out. While the authorities managed to coax Herold from the barn, John Wilkes refused to give up. Before long the barn was on fire and Booth was shot through the back of the neck by Sergeant Boston Corbett. Afterwards they dragged him out of the barn and placed him under a locust tree, where Booth uttered his final words, "Tell my mother I died for my country…Useless, useless…"

This is the story of record about the final days of John Wilkes Booth, the story accepted by nearly every legitimate historian on the subject. It's simple, and has been embedded in our collective consciousness ever since. What is less known, however, is that since the day of the reported shooting, there has been a fiery dispute about whether or not the man shot in the barn was truly John Wilkes Booth.

Traditionalist authors, researchers, and historians hold that the body of the man shot in the barn was definitively identified as John Wilkes Booth by troops who had photos to compare with the body, some of whom had met him in the past. They also claim the corpse was identified as John Wilkes Booth onboard the *USS Montauk*, an ironclad warship in the Washington Navy Yard by, among others, Dr. John Frederick May, who had once performed surgery on Booth's neck to remove a tumor. They also point out that the remains were identified as those of John Wilkes Booth by relatives when the government eventually returned the body to his family, several years after the crime. The traditionalists believe the barn was the definitive end of John Wilkes Booth. Case closed. For years, I agreed with them.

Escape theorists, on the other hand, claim the assassin got away through inside political connections that have never been fully exposed. They believe that the death of Booth at the barn is the greatest hoax ever played on the American public. And just like their traditionalist counterparts, escape researchers also have a war chest of evidence to support their claim.

One of the earliest recorded testimonies of Booth's escape came from a Southern attorney named Finis L. Bates. In 1907, Bates published a controversial book about an unusual loner he knew in Grandberry, Texas, decades earlier by the name of John St. Helen. In the book, Bates detailed how over the course of their acquaintance St. Helen confessed his real name, in truth, was John Wilkes Booth, even though it had been many years since Booth's death was codified.

Bates went on to describe how, years after he lost contact with St. Helen, he was called to identify the body of a man by the name of "David E. George," who had committed suicide in Enid, Oklahoma, only to discover the body was his old acquaintance, John St. Helen, or as he had called himself, John Wilkes Booth. After no legitimate heir surfaced to claim the mysterious corpse, Bates had it mummified, as proof the assassin survived. In 1930 a group of doctors in Chicago, Illinois, examined this same mummy and concluded it was, in fact, John Wilkes Booth.

Similar to the way mainstream culture pokes fun at 9/11 truthers and Bin Laden conspiracy theorists, so do establishment scholars dismiss the legend of the mummy. After the Chicago examination, it became a touring carnival act billed as "John Wilkes Booth, himself, Murderer of Abraham Lincoln." The mummy was sold and re-sold so many times it became a laughing stock, until it disappeared sometime in the late seventies. This scorn would be turned on its head, however, after researchers exhumed the remains of Edwin Booth. At least that's what Daniel thought. He was going to be there to chronicle it. The plans had been in the works for some time.

For years a team of escape researchers had been planning a scientific experiment, they believed, could prove beyond a shadow of a doubt that John Wilkes Booth got away. The idea was to dig up Edwin's grave, take a sample of his DNA, and then compare it with a sample of the man shot in the barn. If the DNA matched, the government could prove they shot the right man at Garrett's barn all along. If the DNA did not match, however, then there would be conclusive proof, once and for all, that John Wilkes Booth did not die at the barn like the history books tell us.

In theory, the experiment was simple, but for years it had been stuck in limbo because the only testable remains of the man shot in the barn are three cervical vertebrae samples extracted from the corpse during the autopsy onboard the *Montauk* in 1865. They're currently displayed in the Anatomical Collection at the National Museum of Health and Medicine, and for years the museum had refused to allow researchers to test them. Frankly, I thought the day would never come. But sure enough, on that freezing winter afternoon, Daniel told me it was finally going to happen. Somehow Nate Orlowek, the lead researcher of the project, managed to convince Congressman Calvin A. Christopher of Maryland to throw his weight behind the proposal, and now it looked as though the moment of truth was in sight.

"This guy is super powerful," Daniel swore. "There is no way they'll oppose him. He's going to be the next Speaker of the House. If the museum doesn't agree, he could slash their budget and put them out of business."

"So when will you know for sure?" I asked him.

"We should find out within the next few days," he said.

Over the course of many hours, Daniel talked extensively about the congressman and the proposal and Nate and the exhumation.

"Nate says, once we get permission, things should move pretty quickly. The exhumation could happen within a few months, although the team wants to be sensitive about the exact date. He said they're not sure if it should be done before or after the anniversary of Lincoln's death. They don't want to insult his memory or anything."

The more he spoke, the looser and more passionate he got. One moment he looked like Edwin, the next he morphed into John. It was astonishing how much he simultaneously resembled both brothers. He was going to be the next Bob Woodward or Edward Snowden. He saw it all so clearly. He recited the information to me like a meditation.

"For Christ's sake," he said, "if that test determines they were not related, and Booth, in fact, got away, it would change everything. It would be the most sensational cover-up in U.S. history. I mean, if this is true, Jesus Christ, aliens and flying saucers might also be true. What else might the government be hiding from us?"

At the time, I thought he was delusional. His dopamine levels were off the chart. I didn't totally disagree with him. A discovery of that magnitude truly would be monumental, but what good would it do? If there really was a secret cabal behind the assassination, the current government couldn't be held accountable. It was a hundred and fifty years ago. It's not like it would bring Lincoln back to life. But at that point, Daniel didn't want to hear it. The story and all of its potential had overcome him. All questions would ultimately be answered in due course and then the end would justify the means.

From this point on I remember very little. Around and around we went the rest of the afternoon, drinking and smoking, while Daniel tirelessly lectured, until Rene finally shut down the bar and kicked us out around midnight. I do recall that during a rare intermission in Daniel's diatribe, we found ourselves sitting across the table from Marilyn Betts.

Marilyn is the president of the board, a devoted mistress of the memory of Edwin Booth. Every December she produces a showcase of his greatest soliloquies. It's a grand event. The old-timers take turns bellowing out gut wrenching excerpts from Hamlet, Othello, King Lear, and other Shakespeare favorites. Then everyone lights their pipes and drinks single malts into the wee hours of the morning. Marilyn is one of the few females who sticks it out to the bitter end. I distinctly recall her reaction when Daniel broke the news to her about the "big dig." Mind you, we were all pretty smashed.

"Can you believe it? They're going to dig up Uncle Edwin," he casually announced before biting into a pretzel.

The room seemed to swirl and darken until a spotlight fell on Marilyn's face, which had rapidly turned pale as bleached paper. She wobbled in her seat a moment, and a tear dripped from her eye.

"Why do they have to dig up Edwin? Why?" she abruptly cried.

The outburst took us by surprise.

"Leave the poor man alone," she continued. "Hasn't he been through enough already?"

There was silence. The only motion came from the bubbles in Marilyn's glass of prosecco. Another tear fell.

"Why?" she wept into her glass. "Why can't they dig up one of the other brothers or sisters? Leave the poor man alone. Hasn't he been through enough already?" she repeated. "I just don't understand it."

I tried to comfort her, but it was no use. The whole affair was complicated and confusing, but that did very little to dry poor Marilyn's tears. In her eyes, Edwin was going to be disturbed from his long slumber for yet another Booth freak show.

"When will it end?" she howled. "When will they ever get enough of the Booths?"

It was a valid question. Unfortunately, it couldn't halt the opportunity to uncover perhaps the oldest conspiracy in United States history. There was no going back.

3

ANDREW JOHNSON

A couple days later I got the following email from Daniel.

Hey, Doc,

Good times the other night. I hope you're as stoked as I am. In any case, here's a rough draft of my notes so far on the real story of JWB's death. As you know, I've been working on them for a while. Have a look. I'm eager to hear what you have to say. I'm thinking of building my narrative around your perspective.

I was now officially a part of his story. I suppose it made sense. I was a convenient counterpoint to all the wild speculation, a true skeptic of all farfetched conspiracy theories, and a traditionalist believer in John Wilkes Booth's death at the barn.

You're perfect! You've been a member of The Players for years. You know most all of the characters. You're a doctor...If I can convince you, I can convince anyone...

I chuckled at the thought, but it's true. I had known most everyone involved for years. At one point or another, they all came through the club. What if they were able to pull it off? I wouldn't want to miss out on it. And it's not like I had anything better going on. So I read through his notes. I have divided them up among the following pages for your review.

I warn you ahead of time, many of Daniel's assertions are provocative. No doubt, they will be highly controversial, particularly his indictment of President Andrew Johnson and Secretary of War Edwin Stanton. As for the veracity of his claims, I cannot speak with any authority. I never got to see a bibliography.

❧

(Daniel's Notes)

Andrew Johnson came into this world on the third-to-last day of 1808, in Raleigh, North Carolina, less than two months before Abraham Lincoln. In many ways these two men shared a similar upbringing.

Both were born in the South into poverty. Both lost a parent at a very young age. Both received little to no formal education and taught themselves how to read. Both men moved away from their home states and defied all odds to become President of the United States. But while the arc of their respective trajectories might appear – looking down from the moon – to have mirrored one another on their paths to the Oval Office, these two American presidents could not have been more diametric opposites. It's not a stretch to say Johnson was Lincoln's alter ego.

A perfect example of how different these presidents were can be found in the polls. Whether conducted by journalists, scholars, or historians, Lincoln is nearly always ranked the greatest president in U.S. history. Johnson, meanwhile, is perpetually ranked the worst. He was, after all, the first president in history to be impeached. But a deeper, more insightful understanding can be gleaned by tracking the different paths these men took from their mutually unfortunate beginnings.

Throughout Johnson's childhood, he was mercilessly teased and ostracized because of his low social standing. His father was a stable keeper and his mother a seamstress. Poor white trash, they called him. But when Johnson's father died, things got worse. The family had no money. Andrew's mother was forced to bind him as an apprentice to a tailor, a fate akin to indentured servitude. But as oppressive as the apprenticeship may have been, the experience ultimately came with a silk lining. It equipped young Andrew with a respectable trade that would get him out of North Carolina and, as soon as he had the chance, he escaped from bondage. And here is where the first major divergence between Lincoln and Johnson begins. While Lincoln veered North in his journey to self-improvement, Johnson plunged deeper south. The South was his destiny.

In South Carolina and Georgia, Johnson found work as a tailor. After a few years, he made his way to Greenville, Tennessee where, upon his first swallow of whiskey at the local saloon, he learned that the old town tailor was looking to retire and was only waiting for someone to buy him out. The timing was perfect for Johnson. With the modest sum of money he'd managed to save since fleeing North Carolina, Johnson bought the old tailor's business without hesitation. Just as Illinois adopted their beloved son, Abraham Lincoln, so Tennessee welcomed Johnson with open arms. The fledgling Southern state gave Johnson a wife, five children, and a platform for an unparalleled career.

Unlike Lincoln, however, who developed empathy and compassion for those less fortunate throughout his many years of toil and struggle, when Johnson finally made it to the top, he turned his back on them. Instead of carrying out Lincoln's mission to abolish slavery, Johnson did all he could to uphold the vile institution, an especially hypocritical stance when you consider that he, himself, found his own servitude – mild in comparison – unbearable and had to escape.

Over the years, Johnson formulated strong opinions on the subject of slavery, and was unabashed in sharing them. And the rich Southern clientele he tailored to was an appreciative audience. They encouraged him. He was a charismatic young man who reminded them of their beloved hero Andrew Jackson. Indeed, Johnson and "Old Hickory" shared many common beliefs, most notably, those pertaining to states' rights, the American Indian, and the expansion of slavery.

Before long, the young tailor was elected mayor of Greenville. From there, he made his way into the Tennessee legislature, before serving five terms in the U.S. House of Representatives. Then in 1857, after two terms as Governor of the state, Johnson was elected to the U.S. Senate, where he would later pull off one of the most daring political maneuvers in the nation's history.

In 1861, when Tennessee seceded from the Union, Johnson became the only Southern Senator not to resign his office during the Civil War. Because Johnson reportedly supported the Federal government, but at the same time was pro-slavery, he was lauded for the ploy. Johnson was seen as a compromiser with the foremost interests of the nation at heart. He instantly became the leading voice of the Democratic Party.

For his allegiance, President Lincoln rewarded Johnson by appointing him the Military Governor of Tennessee. Three years later, ostensibly in the spirit of bi-partisanship, the National Union Party nominated him to be Lincoln's vice-presidential running mate in the election of '64. Little did Lincoln know, as he was poetically laying out his vision for the future, his sly Southern counterpart harbored starkly different motives.

When Lincoln and Johnson were declared the victors in a landslide over Democrats George McClellan and George Pendleton, the vice president-elect was 56 years old, but looked much older. Though always impeccably dressed, Johnson was a heavy drinker and smoker and, by then, the years of abuse had caught up with him. His neck and body had stiffened. The bourbon and tobacco had carved deep wrinkles in his hardened face and, whether drunk or hung-over, Johnson was nearly always irritable. Power was the only force that could soothe him. Johnson became deranged by this single ambition. His thirst for revenge, to prove all those who mocked him in his past wrong, was ever present in his manners and speech.

Of course, none of these characteristics did much to endear him to Lincoln, quite the contrary. Ever since Johnson showed up to his inauguration, reeking of bourbon, and delivered the most intoxicated speech in presidential history, Lincoln had been appalled by his partner. But, by that point, it was too late. Johnson could care less what the president thought of him.

(DANIEL'S NOTES)
JOHN WILKES BOOTH

On April 14, 1865, the Vice President held a secret meeting at the Kirkwood Hotel in Washington, D.C. Conveniently located just down the street from the White House, the hotel had been Johnson's Washington residence since he moved to the capital, less than two months earlier. Outside it was a glorious spring morning. The smell of blooming flowers was in the air. But inside Room 126 the air was stuffy and stale. On that morning Johnson stared directly into the eyes of John Wilkes Booth, as if trying to read his soul. Would Booth follow orders? Would he have the guts to scrap the original plan in favor of something more desperate, more daring?

The last time Johnson and Booth had met it was to discuss a plan to kidnap President Lincoln for ransom, which would have been a stunning victory for the South. Now that plan had expired. Lee's surrender to Grant at Appomattox the week before had thrown the whole plot into disarray. Richmond had fallen. The war was over.

As Will Browning, the vice president's most trusted aide, debriefed Booth that morning, Johnson anxiously paced around the room in silence. The seething Tennessee tailor was buttoned and tied and strapped and cloaked, from neck to toe, in a finely cut assortment of black fabrics. His long, severely parted, charcoal-colored hair – coupled with his dark, penetrating eyes – made him look demonic. His frustration was apparent. He was fuming and irritable, but wasn't ready to give up the plan just yet. The presidency was so close. He could taste it. No, Johnson was consumed by a single thought that morning and when he couldn't tolerate it any longer he leveled his ire at Booth.

"Will you falter now," he shouted, "at this supreme moment?"

The outburst took Booth by surprise. Was the vice president of the United States saying what he thought he was saying? In four words, Johnson made himself plain as a pistol:

"The president must die!"

Johnson explained that the assassination must, by all necessary means, appear to be an all-out attack on the executive office. To deflect every implication – and to eliminate any potential rivals – a hit had to be placed on Secretary of State William Seward, Secretary of War Edwin Stanton, and the Vice President himself. If all were carried out correctly, Johnson would assume the presidency and the Confederacy would posthumously win the war by that simple fact. The South could still win with a shadow government, he said.

Johnson appealed to Booth's strong Confederate sympathies, and his theatrical ego. He dared the actor to avenge the South's pain. The *brave act would immortalize him in the hearts and minds of his common brethren.*

There's no doubt, Booth was smitten by the idea, but to kill a president? No one had ever succeeded. He confessed that he feared for his safety. He told Johnson the mission would mean almost "certain death" to him. Booth pointed out that he had just been detained at the East Potomac (Navy Yard) bridge when he entered the city, less than an hour before he'd arrived at the Kirkwood. Should Booth carry out the task, he'd surely be captured in minutes. There was no possible escape from the heavily fortified Union capital. Booth also pointed out that General Grant and his wife were supposed to accompany the Lincolns to the theater that night, which would complicate matters further.

"Thou would so jeopardize my life?" said Booth. "I am afraid I cannot entertain such whimsy under these present conditions."

The vice president paused for an uncomfortably long moment then stormed out of the room. Booth and Browning, meanwhile, remained in the room awaiting Johnson's return.

An hour later the vice president returned and told Booth it was done. Everything had been arranged perfectly for him. General Grant's widely advertised appearance at Ford's Theater that night was off. The General and his wife had been unexpectedly called out of town and would not be joining the Lincolns after all. Johnson also made it clear to Booth that no one else he might encounter at the theater would interfere with his task. The path had been cleared.

Furthermore, the vice president assured Booth that afterwards, should he succeed, he would be able to safely flee the capital over the same bridge he passed that morning into the city. General C. C. Augur would see to it that the bridge was unguarded, but, should he encounter any soldiers, Booth was to use the password, "T. B. Road," and he would be understood.

Johnson gave Booth his word that as soon as Lincoln was dead, the would-be-assassin could depend upon the would-be-president entirely to ensure his safety. Johnson would protect him to the end and, if need be, pardon him for the crime he would commit on behalf of his country.

"Excellent," Booth said. "So long as I cross the Mississippi unimpeded, not a living soul shall ever learn about your involvement in this matter."

Booth had this grandiose and melodramatic way of speaking. It was artificial and pretentious and often evoked Shakespeare. "Who bids thee call? I do not bid thee call?" and "Get me a horse! A horse! My kingdom for a horse!" were known to be his favorite lines, which is all rather ironic.

Since his infamous deed, John Wilkes Booth has come to be called a great actor. It's not true. Booth was, indeed, a celebrity, and was truly considered one of the handsomest men on stage in his day, but all he accomplished as an actor he owed entirely to his father, Junius, and his brother Edwin, who built the family name, turning "Booth" into a brand of theatre excellence. Sadly for John, he did not inherit the theatrical genius.

Since entering the family business, he succeeded only at dragging the name through the mud. John was an absolute embarrassment, a novice performer at best, a fact he was well aware of. This self knowl-edge made the actor highly insecure, while at the same time, he culti-vated a dangerous determination to distinguish himself from the rest of his family.

His career was extremely short-lived. It consisted of only a hand-ful of years as a professional, and orbited primarily around theaters in the South. Theater owners could generally rely on a decent audience turnout with the name "Booth" attached to the bill, although even that came into question the more the public became acquainted with John. He was good looking and dashing enough to satisfy a less-sophisticated crowd, but as soon as he began to speak, discerning ears would cringe. Playing Shakespeare's arch-villain, "Richard III," may have been the only exception. Sometimes he was able to fake his way through that part, at least in third-rate cities far from New York. The evil nature of the role suited John's melodramatic style. He could get away with shouting his lines and jumping around sinisterly and, of course, engag-ing in lots of daring sword play, his most notable skill.

As a performer Booth was perhaps best known for his fencing, not because he was so talented, but because he was so unpredictable. Audiences loved to watch Booth swing his blade in the same way NASCAR fans love to see a crash. With Booth, they never knew what was going to happen. At times he was known to become so consumed by the passion of a fight that he would relentlessly attack, puncture, maim, or otherwise injure his supporting actor. The audience mainly came to see what pain the erratic actor might inflict that night. This is how John Wilkes Booth first came to know Vice President Johnson.

They met in 1864 when Johnson was still the Military Governor of Tennessee. Booth was touring out west in the role of "Richard" for a limited-engagement run that stopped in several cities, before parking in Nashville for the last leg of the tour. The production received terrible reviews from its start in Richmond. Attendance was scant. Travel between the various cities was plagued by treacherous weather, and several actors had been injured along the way. At one point, Booth and company were stranded in a blizzard for over a week, which sent John into a maniacal rage. But when they finally arrived in Tennessee, the actor's fortune changed. It was there, on the first day of February, that Booth met the man who would change the course of his life.

Colonel William Browning was nebulously referred to as the close "personal aide" of the Governor. In actuality, he was Andrew Johnson's most trusted advisor and true chief of staff, in addition to being a secret Confederate agent. Dressed in elaborate disguises, Browning bounced from one dark corner of the North to another in the South, then to Canada and everywhere in between, tirelessly jockeying Johnson's agenda. After the opening night performance of Booth's "Richard III" at the Nashville Theater, he found himself in Booth's dressing room conversing merrily into the night.

Booth was well known in the Confederate underworld. Ever since John Brown's attack on Harpers Ferry, he had become an active Southern sympathizer, denouncing Northern tyranny everywhere he went. But until he met Browning, Booth's contributions to the cause were largely self-serving.

Not long after the war began, Booth started a successful shipping operation. Because he was a touring actor, Booth had a war visa, which enabled him to travel freely in and out of the States, as well as across the Atlantic, without raising suspicion. Employing a fleet of junkyard vessels, and a renegade crew of sailors based out of New Brunswick, Booth outmaneuvered the Union naval blockades and smuggled medicine into the Confederacy from Canada, for hefty wartime profits. It was the perfect cover for the actor.

It was from this "side" business that Booth made his fortune. It was also the reason he was visited by Will Browning that evening at the theater. Browning thought Booth might be a useful tool in a developing speculation that could potentially produce very lucrative yields for all involved. Over brandy by the fire that night, he told the profiteering actor all about it.

Living in post-industrial America these days it's easy to overlook just how important cotton as a cash crop was to our country in the nineteenth century. It was the number-one U.S. export, supplying over two-thirds of the world's cotton demand. The economics of cotton were the driving force behind slavery and the Civil War. "King Cotton" is what the Confederacy believed would enable them to win the war and, afterwards, grow a robust economy – rooted in slavery – that would eventually extend southward all the way to Brazil. Demand for cotton throughout Europe, in particular, was high. It was only logical then, Southerners reasoned, that England and France would come to their rescue. All the cotton was in the South. Where else were they going to get it?

What the Confederacy underestimated, however, was the might of the Union's Navy. The North effectively managed to grind the export of cotton from the South to a startling halt, thus cutting off its primary revenue stream. The North then made it clear to England, and France, and Spain, and the rest of Europe, if they wanted cotton, they would have to go through them. The strategy worked.

By 1864 the South was starving. Richmond couldn't afford to buy them food and even if it could, there was no one to supply it. The naval blockades had effectively choked off any food that might come from foreign sources. The Confederacy was being strangled, but still had that dangerous rage of a hungry man with just enough fight left in him to kill.

Wisely, the North remained cautious. After three long years of war, they had also been badly battered. If the North really wanted to knock out the South for good, they needed to hit them with a big stick. This is where "meat for cotton" came in, the grand (and highly covert) plan Browning explained to Booth in his dressing room that cold, winter night.

Because the war had frozen supply, the price of cotton had skyrocketed around the world. In Europe, cotton was going for between ten and twenty times its pre-war price. Not surprisingly, as the war waged on, and shares of the crop continued to surge, Wall Street began to take a serious interest. And, soon enough, they found a way to get in on the action.

Another tangible advantage the North had over the South – although it took years to materialize – was that most of the livestock in the country was in Union territory. Meat was plentiful in the North, and cheap, which was not good for the meat industry. The Union-enforced trade embargo with the Confederacy meant meat suppliers, who before the war were making a healthy living selling to the South, were now sitting on stockpiles of meat. Now "Big Meat" was losing big money.

Recognizing that famine was rapidly setting in on the South, a shrewd group of Northern investors came up with the idea of trading the North's vast reserves of pork for cotton. The plan would be win-win, if they could just figure a way around the embargo.

Before long, the moneymen on Wall Street were talking with Big Meat and Big Cotton, and, shortly thereafter, with politicians and law-makers in Washington about the prospect of a deal. It was simple: once the Confederacy got the meat to feed its Army, the investors would get the cotton, which, in turn, would be shipped off to New York, where it would be auctioned off to eager buyers abroad for a staggering profit.

What sealed the deal for officials in Washington was that the scheme cut them in. The trade would significantly replenish the Union's depleted Treasury. But the plan had to be hushed-up. If word got out that the North was – literally – feeding the war, it would enflame the "Radical" Republicans in Congress.

This is the real reason Andrew Johnson was placed on the ticket with Lincoln in '64. He was the backup plan for the scheme. As surprising as this may seem, what's even more shocking is that the meat-for-cotton scheme was originally hatched by none other than President Abraham Lincoln.

His chief bodyguard in the White House – Ward Lamon – was one of the most influential cotton lobbyists in the country. The two men were close friends in Springfield, where they were partners at the same law firm. Before the war even began, Lamon had told Lincoln the only way the North could win was by securing cotton from the South. Lincoln agreed, but couldn't see how it was possible. With conditions as they were when Browning introduced Booth to Johnson, however, Lincoln was finally ready to act. By that point, he needed to end the war, win reelection, and reconstruct the nation. And to succeed, he needed cash. So Lamon set up the deal.

By July of '64, Congress had paved the way by passing a trade bill that permitted the Federal government to do business with the Confederacy. The rules were straightforward. Any "dealer" who could deliver cotton to the Treasury would be awarded a contract. In exchange for a twenty-five percent tax on the market rate for cotton, the dealers could trade their crop in New York. Theoretically, anyone could get in on the game, but in reality, only one group of entrepreneurs would benefit.

The Confederacy was the only supplier who could deliver sufficient shipments of cotton to make it worthwhile, and the only thing they wanted was meat. This is where Booth came in. To deliver the pork would require out-foxing the Navy. Booth was already a tried and true smuggler. He knew how to sneak past the blockades.

For this reason, Johnson invited Booth to attend a top-secret logistics meeting at the St. Lawrence Hotel in Montreal in October of 1864. Confidential contracts had been drawn up by the Treasury (signed by Lincoln) for twenty million pounds of meat to be delivered throughout the South over the course of a few months.

Booth arrived the night before the meeting and, by the time he checked in at the hotel, everyone in Montreal knew how he felt about Lincoln. The actor was a blabbermouth. He openly blamed the

President for all the South's troubles and would articulate his feelings to anyone who would listen.

To Booth, Lincoln was the reason he was smuggling food to his fellow countrymen. And even though he was a relatively small player in the operation, that didn't stop the actor from expressing his outrage in the private hotel suite where the principals met that crisp autumn afternoon. It was there that he first volunteered to kidnap Lincoln. As appealing as this idea was to many in the room at the time, it nonetheless raised eyebrows, since nobody wanted to be implicated in plot of that magnitude.

Browning stepped in and diffused the awkwardness. He told Booth, for the time being, he should simply focus on getting the meat past the blockades. Then, if down the road there were other complicating factors, they might need to consider a backup plan. But plan A was to avoid it at all costs.

When they left the St. Lawrence that October, everyone had their assignments, and they all went their separate ways. Despite Browning's moderate concern for Booth's sanity, everything was going according to plan. The actor made quick headway in his limited role, until about a week before the election.

Around that time, a secret Union agent intercepted an important piece of intelligence that detailed certain integral parts of the plan, including Lincoln's involvement. As soon as this was discovered, the message was sent immediately to Secretary of War Edwin Stanton. The Secretary was furious and confronted Lincoln at once.

A large and forceful man, weighing three hundred and fifty pounds, Stanton always believed he was mentally superior to the tall and gangly president. Back when Stanton was a practicing attorney in Ohio, he once referred to Lincoln as a "damned, long-armed ape." But as head of the War Department, Stanton was even more blunt, never holding back his frank, unapologetic opinions.

Ideologically, Stanton was strongly aligned with the antislavery Republicans in Congress and tirelessly devoted all his power and resources to stomping the institution out. So when he found out that Lincoln was supporting soldiers who were fighting his troops, Stanton hit the ceiling.

After the secretary chewed out his superior, reprimanding him every which way, the president began to have a change of heart. Stanton was right (and would never forget it). Lincoln had to back down. "Honest Abe" deliberated about it and soon came around to Stanton's way of thinking on the subject, which was to take the cotton outright from the South, by force, without compensation or trade and ship it directly to New York.

Stanton's outrage had a disastrous effect on Booth and the rest of the players. The naval blockades clamped-down hard and detained all meat entering the Confederacy. The pressure was on. Washington and Wall Street, Big Meat and Big Cotton, Browning and Booth, were all stranded in limbo. There was too much at stake. Lincoln had to go. The president was too compromised.

After Lincoln and Johnson won the election, Browning contacted Booth and told him to proceed with the kidnapping plan. Booth was thrilled by the opportunity and began searching for recruits. The plan was to snatch Lincoln and ship him down the Potomac River to Richmond, where he would be ransomed back to the Union for a fortune. In the meantime, Johnson would secure the White House and dismiss Stanton from the War Department and replace him with a stooge, and they'd all be back in business.

The plan seemed promising enough. Unfortunately for the profiteers, by the time it became evident that Booth was completely incompetent as a kidnapper, the war was nearly over, which would send the inflated price of cotton plummeting.

For three months, Booth attempted to nab the president, unsuccessfully. He came close a few times, but never delivered. His accomplices were a bunch of unreliable drunks, in way over their heads. The whole thing had become a farce. By the time spring rolled around, the high command had seen enough. Time was just about up. Millions of pounds of meat were rotting in Union Navy yards. They had to move quickly.

JUNIUS BRUTUS BOOTH

A month or so went by before I heard from Daniel again. I got a call at the club. Rene brought the phone over and told me he had no idea who it was. When I said hello, a Groucho Marx voice asked, "Hey, Doc, who's buried in Grant's Tomb?"

It was Daniel, and it turned out that's exactly where he was. I asked him why I hadn't seen him around the club recently.

"Doc, I don't even know where to begin," he said.

At long last, he told me, official word had come down from the museum authorizing the testing. I'm not sure if your bureau reported on the development. I do recall that a few local papers and television stations picked up on it, but on the whole, the news seemed to pass unnoticed by the general public. In the Booth community, however, bells were ringing.

Immediately, the research team began the paperwork to dig up Edwin at Mount Auburn Cemetery in Cambridge, Massachusetts. For symbolic reasons, they wanted to perform the exhumation on April 26th, the anniversary of John's death at the barn, which drew scathing criticisms from the traditional establishment on their websites, chat rooms, newsletters, and I'm sure in the privacy of their homes.

Daniel, meanwhile, was a man on a mission. Every spare second he had, he was either making a phone call or sending an email, hopping a train or a bus and God knows what else, furiously trying to get all his pre-exhumation notes together. Time was running out.

From inside Grant's mausoleum, he told me he had just interviewed a history professor from Columbia University about the significance of Booth in the post-Civil War era, but that wasn't why he was calling.

"How would you like to join me on my next trip?" he asked.

I chuckled.

"That depends," I said. "What do you have in mind?"

"I can tell you right now, you're gonna love it. Everything's set up already. All you have to do is drive. It'll be loads of fun and, hey, while you're at it, would you mind picking up the bill? I'm dead broke."

How could I resist?

The plan was to first stop in Bel Air, Maryland, where John and Edwin and the rest of their siblings were born. Daniel had an appointment with a woman named Joan Stevens who supposedly had evidence that Sam Houston Jr. helped harbor John in Texas after his escape. It's common knowledge that Sam's father, Sam Houston Sr., founding father of the Lone Star State, and John's father, Junius Brutus Booth, had been the best of friends in their youth. According to Daniel, Mrs. Stevens had agreed to furnish him with the necessary proof, which would have been a compelling piece of evidence for the escape researchers.

After this, we would then drive to Green Mount Cemetery in Baltimore where everyone, except Edwin, is buried. Daniel wanted to snap a few photos at sunset for the book. From there, we'd spend the night in Baltimore before heading to Silver Spring the next morning to meet with a curator from the Museum of Health and Medicine. Then for the climax of the trip, we'd finish up with the official "Booth Escape Tour," the one where he dies at the barn.

Of course, in between all these activities, Daniel would be meeting and interviewing various oddballs on the street to get more pre-exhumation quotes. And then there was a stop at the Mexican Embassy in Washington thrown in, too, for an unrelated Beacon story about Mexican cooking in Brooklyn. It was part of his sabbatical.

I picked up Daniel in Brooklyn a little after ten in the morning on the fourteenth of March. When I pulled up to his building he was already waiting out front. He was a spinning mass of energy.

"You ready for the trip of a lifetime?" he asked.

"Who wouldn't be?" Then, before I knew it, Tito Puente was blazing from the speakers as we soared across the Verrazano.

Around the time we passed Atlantic City, Daniel asked me what I thought of his notes. I could tell he was eager for a response. I told him his notes were very interesting, but admitted, I found some it hard to swallow.

"Incidentally," I asked him, "do you have any proof to back all of this up?"

"Doc, that's just the tip of the iceberg," he assured me. "You wouldn't believe all the evidence Nate and the rest of the team have uncovered."

I took him at his word and continued to withhold judgment. The test would sort it all out before long, I thought.

"Well, I look forward to seeing it," I said, and we left it at that, for the time being.

By my watch, we arrived in Bel Air, Maryland, at exactly 1:05 p.m. The sun was bright and the temperature unusually warm for March. Main Street was sleepy now, but the town's ten thousand residents would have made it a thriving metropolis back when Junius Brutus Booth built his home there in the eighteen hundreds.

Back then there was no town. Bel Air was the wilderness, precisely what Junius wanted. It was the perfect place to raise his illegitimate family. The plan worked for many years. Hidden away on an isolated farm, far from his wife back in England, Mary Ann Holmes gave birth to ten of Junius's children, including Edwin and John.

Junius Booth was a strong patriarch in both character and influence. He was the first thespian in the family. Born in London, England, into an ordinary middle-class family, he was captivated early by the prospect of fame and fortune on the stage. By the time he was seventeen he had committed to a career in acting and, apparently, had a knack for the trade. Within a few years he earned a reputation for being one of the foremost tragedians in all of London, and eventually struck up a bonafide rivalry with Edmund Kean, at the time considered the greatest actor in Britain.

By the age of nineteen, Junius married Marie Christine "Adelaide" Delannoy, a Belgian socialite ten years his senior. Soon after, they had two children, one of whom, Richard Brutus Booth, lived past the age of one. For years Adelaide and the young children tagged along with Junius while he toured Europe performing, but when the opportunity came for the actor to travel to the states, Lady Delannoy declined to join him, opting instead for the comfort of her new home in England. It was at this juncture that Junius's life took perhaps its sharpest turn.

The world will never know how he felt as he bid his wife farewell. Junius promised to write and send money, then kissed her and hugged her goodbye. He neglected, however, to tell her that a gorgeous young flower girl would be joining him on his voyage across the Atlantic, and that he would never return to England again. Sadly, I have the misfortune of knowing how Junius felt when Mrs. Booth eventually found out. I went through a similar ordeal when my wife discovered my infidelities. It wasn't pretty.

6

TUDOR HALL

It took a little effort to find Tudor Lane, the road that leads to the former Booth homestead, now a non-profit historical society owned by Harford County. It's at the outer edge of town. The paved roadway is still lined with giant elms, but the dense Maryland forest that once bordered the narrow dirt lane has been replaced by a sprawling housing development. At the end of the road, however, when you begin to roll down the old carriageway, you still feel a cozy sense of seclusion. The landscaping tastefully obstructs the surrounding stockades of vinyl siding.

We pulled up to the main building in the center of the property, the storied old cottage Junius called "Tudor Hall," which, incidentally, was built by the same man who built Ford's Theater. The whole property is immaculately kept. There's a pond and a springhouse and a barn and a couple other small structures that are all still intact and shaded by old trees. There's also a long meadow and an expansive garden. Gardening was said to have been Junius's favorite pastime.

While Daniel went to the front door, my mind drifted off into the bucolic scenery. For a few moments I felt like I was Junius. I quickly snapped out of it when Daniel returned to the car.

"How strange," he said. "They couldn't possibly be closed."

"You sure she's expecting you?" I asked.

"Of course I'm sure," Daniel reassured me. "I called her yesterday to confirm." He then suggested we follow the driveway around the rear of the property to have a look.

I rounded the bend and discovered a small lot at the back of the house, but there was no sign of Mrs. Stevens there either. I parked and we both got out. Daniel went to the back door and rapped on it loudly, hoping he might awaken some sleepy housekeeper who might hear him and cheerfully answer the door. That's the way his mind worked. I meanwhile surveyed the surrounding yard, wondering if we'd missed some vital checkpoint.

I didn't see anything at first. The whole scene resembled a nineteenth century landscape painting. But as I roamed the perimeter of the house, I glimpsed a vehicle parked behind one of the barns at the far edge of the property. As I set out in that direction across the long meadow, Daniel caught up with me.

"You see anyone Doc?" he asked.

"I'm not sure," I said.

As we got closer, the vehicle came into better view, but when we got within about fifty feet of it, we stopped, dumbstruck.

Sitting on the hood of a large black pick-up truck were two stunning figures. One was a pale-skinned blonde, the other a darker-complexioned brunette. They were casually smoking what appeared to be a joint. I had a surreal feeling that I was dreaming.

"What should we do?" Daniel asked.

It was unusual to see Daniel paralyzed like that. He always acted quickly and decisively.

"I don't know," I told him. "Say hello, I suppose."

"Right," he said. And then after a moment, as if waking from a trance, he confidently sprung into action. I followed somewhat more self-consciously.

"Hi, there," Daniel said as we approached them. "Do you ladies work here?"

They both smiled and the blonde answered, "No."

"I have an appointment with Joan Stevens. Have you seen her?"

The blonde shook her head. "I don't think they're open today," she said before raising the joint to her lips and inhaling.

I was shocked by how flagrantly they were smoking in front of us. They didn't know us from Edwin. We could have been under-cover cops for all they knew.

"Really?" Daniel continued. "Because I looked on the website and it says they're open until six."

"Yeah, well," she said, exhaling and then taking another drag, "sometimes no one shows up."

"What brings you here then?"

The girls looked at each other and smiled.

"Well, it's a great place to have a smoke without anyone bothering you."

"I see," said Daniel.

I didn't know what to make of them. The way they sat there and casually smoked their joint, the way they talked so glibly, the way they were dressed so seductively in their light patterned dresses, they were like a pair of high-class call girls, yet somehow they seemed too relaxed, too indifferent, to be on the prowl. With a hypnotic gesture of her hand, the blonde passed the joint to her friend.

"You're not going to tell on us are you?" she said.

"Us?" said Daniel. "Of course not."

"You want some?"

Daniel looked at me.

"What do you say, Doc?"

"You go ahead," I told him. "I'm alright for now."

"You're a doctor?" the blonde said trying to put it all together in her stoned mind.

"Was a doctor. I'm retired now."

"Oh. I see. Well, congratulations."

The way they phrased their sentences made me wonder if English wasn't their second language, even though they appeared to be as American as cherry pie.

"Is it important, your meeting, that is?" the brunette asked.

"Important?" Daniel repeated with a chuckle, considering the brunette for the first time. "I guess you could say so."

The brunette returned the joint to the blonde who passed it to Daniel. He paused and considered it for a long moment before taking a deep drag. He held it for an absurd amount of time. After he exhaled, he took another puff then handed it back to the blonde and thanked her. Then an awkward silence descended. The ladies just sat there, smoking, with their eyes fixed intently on Daniel, who looked deep in thought. It was dreadfully uncomfortable. I tried to chime in, but no words came. Finally, Daniel broke the silence with a refreshingly upbeat tone.

"Do you mind if I take a photograph of you ladies?" he asked.

They both paused and telepathically consulted each other. The blonde then smiled and said, "Sure. I don't see why not."

"Great," he said, and pulled out his camera and proceeded to take several shots of them on the hood of the truck. All the while he kept reassuring them by saying, "Perfect," and "Great" and "Excellent."

When he finished, the brunette asked him what he was going to do with the pictures. He paused. I could see his mind wrestling with how to answer. In the end, he couldn't resist. Whether it was because he wanted to impress them, or because it was truly the only thing he knew how to talk about at that point, Daniel spilled the beans and told them about his book. Shortly after he told them his theory about the barn, he abruptly stopped.

"You'll have to pardon me," he said. "I'm extremely embarrassed. I don't even know your names."

The blonde smiled and her eyes seemed to twinkle when she said, "I'm Monica." The sparkle lasted until her friend said, "And I'm Francesca."

Given the circumstances of our meeting, I was a bit reluctant to give out my name. I was already disgraced enough. Daniel, however, didn't flinch. He gave them his whole name, middle initial and all.

"What a nice name," Francesca said in response. "It's very powerful. Is it a family name?"

"Actually, it is," Daniel quickly replied. "He's Daniel Boland Senior," he said, referring to me.

"Oh, how cute," Francesca said. "A father son adventure."

Yet again, Daniel had surprised me. Not that I was offended. I was flattered. I had been starting to think of Daniel as a son. I hadn't spoken to my own son since the divorce. I often wonder if I'll ever speak to him again.

After they finished the joint, Daniel suggested we all relocate to the front porch of the house, in case Joan or anyone else who could let us in arrived. On the porch, Daniel continued his dissertation. I thought for sure he was going to drive them away with it, but once again I was proven wrong. They genuinely seemed interested.

"There are just so many holes in the fairytale ending I can hardly keep them in my head," he said. "For starters, doesn't it stand to reason that if the government really believed the man they killed was Booth, they would have taken some pictures? The one photo they took was immediately destroyed the moment it was taken, never again seen on God's green earth. And no one knows how or why."

"That's not suspicious," Monica said sarcastically, as she lit up another joint.

"But more than the photo," Daniel continued, "why didn't they have anyone who knew Booth in childhood, or adulthood for that matter, identify the body so that they could put the issue to rest forever? Of the dozen or so people who ID'd him on the warship in the Navy Yard, no one was a close friend or relative. That's because the government knew that body wasn't Booth."

As always, Daniel made a compelling argument. He was grooming himself for his press tour when his book finally hit the shelves. With each recitation of the evidence, he got smoother and smoother. And the girls seemed to be eating it up.

"But the most persuasive evidence, in my opinion, that Booth got away, is the fact that when Davey Herold supposedly gave himself up and came out of the barn, his first words were, 'The man in there is not John Wilkes Booth.' "

At this point I had to interrupt him. Maybe I was trying to show off for the ladies myself because they seemed so interested. But the truth is, the Herold statement never held water with me and I had sat by quietly and listened to this story way too many times to let it pass by one more time.

"No one has ever shown me any solid proof to back that up," I said. "Herold mentioned Booth's name over a dozen times when he debriefed the authorities afterward."

Daniel seemed a bit surprised by my reaction, but he knew better. He knew how skeptical I was about all this circumstantial evidence.

"That's because you put all your faith in the official report," he said, "which was totally bogus. Herold was pressured into changing his statement, as were many others, because the government wanted to wrap up the case as quickly as possible, and the troops wanted their reward money. The conspirators, including Herold, were tortured in prison. Herold thought he could save his life by telling them what they wanted to hear. So he did. Case in point, Doctor May."

This was always his clincher. Dr. John Frederick May was the Washington surgeon who participated in the government autopsy. He removed a tumor from the back of Booth's neck some years before the assassination.

"Doctor May knew immediately it wasn't Booth," he said, "but the pressure from the War Department got to him. Stanton, or rather Colonel Baker, made it very clear to him that he better go along with the program. Why else would he say for the record, 'There is no resemblance in that corpse to Booth, nor can I believe it to be that of him. Oh, but on closer examination, yes, that's definitely John Wilkes Booth?' Signed John Frederick May. The whole thing is preposterous."

He had a point. May's statement has always been puzzling, but Daniel and his fellow escape theorists, I thought, always played on it way too much. It was circumstantial at best. A bit annoyed, I looked at my watch. It was three o'clock. Nearly two hours had passed without a sign of Joan Stevens.

"I don't know how to break it to you," Monica finally said, "but I don't think your friend is coming."

Daniel was conflicted about how to proceed.

"We could break in and see if she's in there hiding," Francesca suggested.

I laughed. It never occurred to me she might actually be serious. That was all we needed, the cops showing up and getting thrown into a paddy wagon.

"I think we'll pass on that option," Daniel said, much to my relief.

I'm sure he thought about it though, however briefly. He was always calculating. This story was the reason for his existence. I suspect, however, he weighed the risk-reward factor and concluded he had a better chapter on his hands with the girls. He could always come back for Sam Houston.

"Hey, you ladies aren't interested in driving down with us to Baltimore, are you?" he asked. "We're gonna check out a graveyard."

"Funny you should ask," Monica answered. "We were planning on heading to Baltimore tonight anyway. What do you say Francesca? Should we tag along with these two misfits?"

Daniel laughed.

"Who's grave are we going to see?" asked Francesca.

"Who else?"

And with that, the girls skipped off to their 4x4. When I was sure they were out of earshot, I couldn't help but express my concerns.

"Hey," I said quietly, "are you sure you want these girls tagging along with us? I mean, we don't know anything about them. And I have to confess, the whole vibe here has me a bit on edge."

"Doc, don't worry so much," he assured me. "These ladies are a blessing. Just look at them."

Before we could discuss it any further, the girls pulled up in front of us and Monica rolled down her window.

"You guys ready to burn?" she said with a big smile.

Minutes later I kicked the car into high gear. A few clouds had rolled in, but it was still mostly sunny. I lowered the roof and Daniel's long, black locks began to swirl around in the wind. On one marked occasion I glanced at him from the corner of my eye and, I swear, he looked like a spitting image of John Wilkes Booth, minus the mustache. Of course it was my imagination having a laugh at my expense, but it went beyond just looks. In that instant, I gleaned just how monomaniacal and brooding Daniel could sometimes be. If you asked me for a clinical classification, I would have diagnosed Daniel with mild to moderate NPD, or Narcissistic Personality Disorder. Though not nearly as extreme as John, I never quite looked at Daniel the same way again.

7

(DANIEL'S NOTES)
THE GREAT ESCAPE

At 10:16 P.M. John Wilkes Booth busted out of the backstage door of Ford's Theater into Baptist Alley. In the dark alley, Joseph Burroughs, a young stagehand who had no idea what Booth had just done, was holding the reigns of the assassin's horse. When Burroughs noticed Booth hobbling toward him, he asked the actor what happened. But Booth was in no mood for questions. He responded by violently kicking the unsuspecting stagehand in the shins and pummeling him in the head, before mounting his horse.

As Booth raced down the alley to F Street, he was joined by his sidekick, who had been guarding the escape route to make sure the path was clear. Contrary to popular belief, this man was not David E. Herold.

Herold had been assigned to assist Lewis Powell in killing Secretary of State William Seward. He was supposed to be the lookout and getaway man. But when the moment of truth came, and Powell entered the Secretary's house, Herold got cold feet and abandoned the mission, heading home toward the Chesapeake Bay, where he hoped to sleep the episode off, as if it were all a bad dream.

Booth's true accomplice was a man by the name of Edwin Henson. Henson had assisted the actor multiple times over the years in his smuggling operation and various other schemes. Unfortunately for Davey Herold, he resembled Henson too closely the night of the assassination.

Both men were roughly the same height, both had the same slight build, similar brown hair, and youthful open face, and both of their names began with the same two letters (and were both six letters long). They also happened to rent their horses from the same Pumphrey's stable on E Street that same morning. And considering both men failed to return their horses to the stable that night, it's easy to understand how John Fletcher – the stable foreman, and key witness to Booth and "Herold's" escape – mixed the two men up.

It was pitch black when Fletcher caught sight of Henson's shadow galloping past him that night. What really caught Fletcher's eye was his horse, who, at that point, was hours past due, and heading in the opposite direction of the stable. Fletcher chased after Booth and Henson, having no idea that he was actually chasing after Lincoln's assassin, or that Lincoln had been shot at all.

Fletcher followed the assailants all the way to the Navy Yard Bridge. Much to his dismay, by the time he arrived at the military checkpoint, Booth and Henson were halfway across the Potomac. When Fletcher asked the guard on duty if he could pursue the two men and retrieve his horse, the stable foreman was denied. The guard had received specific instructions not to let anyone pass in or out of the city, unless they announced the secret password, "T.B. Road," of course.

Traditional historians delight in describing Fletcher's short-sighted dread of breaking the news to his boss about the lost horse. As he left the Navy Yard Bridge he was, indeed, quite distraught, oblivious to the role he would eventually play in identifying the culprits of the most sensational assassination in U.S. history. Few scholars acknowledge that Fletcher got it wrong, much to the relief of Henson.

Meanwhile, as Booth and Henson traveled deeper into the swamplands of Maryland, Secretary of War Edwin Stanton found himself sinking deeper and deeper into a swamp of his own.

Across the street from Ford's Theater, on the second floor of the Peterson House, where the dying President lay stretched diagonally across his improvised deathbed, Stanton had his hands full. The public was panicked. No one had ever succeeded in killing an American President before. Now Stanton alone was responsible for picking up the pieces. He knew all along what was going to happen, but now that the moment had arrived, he was overwhelmed. What a tragic end, Stanton thought.

He had once been one of Lincoln's harshest critics. Stanton had sworn an oath to his father as a young boy to fight slavery until his dying breath. Abolition was the only virtuous path forward, as far as Stanton was concerned. In Lincoln's early years as a politician, Stanton didn't believe he was fighting hard enough for the cause. In 1860, he opposed Lincoln's bid for the White House. But in time, Lincoln won him over.

After witnessing the president's strength and resolve grow with the abolitionist movement throughout the war years, Stanton had a change of heart. He began to admire Lincoln's intellectual curiosity and unique leadership style. But now that the North had won, Stanton was not about to let the South reincorporate without consequence, the way Lincoln suggested. In Stanton's mind, the Commander-in-Chief could not be trusted after the meat-for-cotton debacle.

Johnson, on the other hand, was talking tough, feeding the Secretary exactly what he wanted to hear. For months the vice president had been crafting his rhetoric. And to deflect any involvement of his own in the meat-for-cotton scheme, Johnson had Will Browning leak the secret document implicating Lincoln to Stanton. The tactic —causing an irreparable rift between the president and the secretary — worked.

When Stanton confronted Johnson with evidence of the president's subversive act, Johnson was ready to tell him what he wanted to hear. He assured Stanton that such actions would never stand in his administration. In fact, Johnson promised if he were president, he would appoint Stanton to the Supreme Court so that he could rewrite the constitution as he saw fit, abolishing slavery forever, and severely punishing the South. As a pre-eminent law scholar, Stanton knew that presidents come and go, but a Supreme Court appointment is for life. This is how Stanton became involved in the assassination plot. And on the night of April 14, he had his work cut out for him.

To begin with he had to deal with the perpetrators of the crime. They had to be swiftly brought to justice. Of course, he couldn't pursue Booth. Stanton had been forewarned that Booth had evidence, at the ready, that would incriminate everyone involved should anything unfortunate happen to him. Now Stanton had to create a distraction large enough to divert any unwanted attention from his office.

The minute he was called to the president's side, Stanton made sure that word spread quickly over the military's telegraph network that the city was in lockdown mode. A general alarm was sounded to alert military commanders that no one was allowed in or out of the capital, except of course for Booth.

"Every exertion has been made to prevent the escape of the murderer," Stanton dictated, in one of the many telegraphs he sent the night of the assassination. "Make immediate arrangements for guarding thoroughly every avenue leading into Baltimore, and if possible arrest J. Wilkes Booth, the murderer of President Lincoln."

Stanton knew that dispatching troops immediately, before accurate intelligence came in, was key to covering his back and manufacturing confusion. He mobilized the Navy. He sent battalions of troops to the north, to the west, to the east, in every direction but the most likely route Booth would have taken: the south.

One of the earliest commanders to be ordered north was Colonel Thompson at Darnestown, just northwest of the capital. He replied to the order by telegraph at 11:30 P.M. (an hour and fifteen minutes after Booth pulled the trigger). Thompson's message was unmistakable:

"THE ASSASSINS ARE SUPPOSED TO HAVE ESCAPED TOWARD MARYLAND."

But the message was in vain. By 4 A.M. the next morning, while colonels and generals were marshaling squadrons of troops on a bogus chase in the opposite direction, Booth was thirty miles away from the capital, safe and sound, at Dr. Mudd's house. Only one small cavalry unit was sent in Booth's direction. It's impossible to imagine that the architect of the great Northern victory could have been so incompetent.

In reality, Stanton was anything but incompetent. At the same time Dr. Mudd opened his door to Booth and Henson, Stanton called on the only man who could help him clean up the mess, a high-ranking officer he had recently fired from a key position in his War Department. The man – Colonel Lafayette C. Baker – received the urgent telegraph at the Astor House Hotel in New York, where he was staying on the morning of April 15th.

"Come here immediately," Stanton commanded, "and find the murderer of our President."

In many ways, Colonel Baker was the J. Edgar Hoover of his day. He was the director of the National Detective Police, a counter-intelligence agency and predecessor to the FBI, that is, until Stanton discovered he was spying on him and sacked the colonel from his post. A master spy, Baker had information, and dirt, on everyone, which made him very dangerous. But during those dark hours immediately following the assassination, Stanton understood that the only person who could figure out a solution to the Booth conundrum was his former chief detective. Yet Baker did not return to Washington as expressly as the secretary commanded.

Unbeknownst to Stanton, Baker was secretly a majority partner in the "Henry J. Eager Company," one of the prime movers behind the meat-for-cotton coup, and before he could leave New York, he had to close a very profitable business deal. It involved blackmailing one of his partners, the unlucky Robert D. Watson, a meat man from Kentucky, who mistakenly put his trust in Lafayette Baker. By the time the colonel arrived in Washington the following morning, Watson was ruined, but at least he got to live.

Meanwhile, Andrew Johnson made his play for the highest office in the land. At 10 A.M. on Easter Sunday, 1865, in his private suite at the Kirkwood Hotel, Johnson was sworn in as the seventeenth President of the United States by Chief Justice Salmon Chase. Afterward, those in attendance remarked how peculiar it was that in his speech, which lasted five minutes, Johnson made no mention of Lincoln, at all. Not once did he reference his slain predecessor's name, his character, his accomplishments, his contributions, nothing. In contrast, he did reference himself upwards of twenty times.

"My past public life, which has been long and laborious," Johnson said, "has been founded – as I in good conscience believe – upon the great principle of right which lies at the base of all things. I must be permitted to say, if I understand the feelings of my own heart, I have long labored to ameliorate and alleviate the conditions of the great mass of the American people. Toil and an honest advocacy of the great principles of free government have been my lot. The duties have been mine, the consequence God's."

Witnesses of the event were flabbergasted by his egotism. The distinguished Senator from New Hampshire, John P. Hale, observed, "Johnson seemed willing to share the glory of his achievements with his Creator, but utterly forgot that Mr. Lincoln had any share or credit."

Days later, of course, Johnson would talk a good talk about bringing the perpetrators of the dreadful act to ultimate justice. Indeed, he was confident Baker and Stanton would work out all the details in the end, which is exactly what happened.

As soon as Baker arrived on the scene, he laid his terms coldly on the War Secretary's desk. They were non-negotiable. Baker knew how badly Stanton needed him. And after the way he had been dismissed as chief of the NPD, Stanton was going to have to pay a premium price.

Baker insisted the government pony up an unprecedented amount of cash for the capture of Lincoln's killers. The money, theoretically, would be up for grabs to any man, woman, or child who could deliver Booth and his accomplices. This would not only bolster public opinion that the War Department was doing everything possible to catch the culprits, but also create further mayhem, as hundreds of bounty hunters and fortune seekers would attempt to cash in on the prize. The feverish public pursuit, Baker speculated, would naturally propagate misinformation and lead to a flood of false claims that would ultimately shield the department's internal operation. Stanton agreed and, in the end, they settled on $100,000—the rough equivalent of $3 million in today's money.

The second – and most important – term was that Baker would collect the reward money himself. It was a relatively small price to pay, Stanton reasoned. All that mattered was the result: Booth had to be dead in the public's mind. This was exactly the type of job that Baker excelled at. In this case, he had been planning the job for over six months behind Stanton's back.

Baker was the true mastermind behind the Lincoln coup. Setting up a fall guy for Booth was part of his job description from the very beginning. The minute the kidnapping plan had been authorized, he began a search for Booth's understudy. And the moment he laid eyes on Captain James William Boyd, he knew he had his man.

A Confederate secret agent himself, Boyd was captured by Union forces in Jackson, Tennessee and imprisoned there in 1863. Not long after he was thrown in prison, Boyd learned that his wife Caroline back in Kentucky was sick and dying from consumption. Concerned about what would become of his seven children should his wife die, Boyd wrote numerous letters to Governor Johnson begging to be pardoned so that he could take care of his family. By the fall of 1864, Will Browning finally paid Captain Boyd a visit. Afterward, Browning promptly contacted Baker and informed him about the prisoner's uncanny physical characteristics.

He was the same height as Booth. He had the same style hair and mustache as Booth. His build was like Booth's. His face looked like Booth's. True, Boyd did have a few more freckles. Booth's complexion was startlingly pale and smooth. And Boyd's hair color was a little closer to brown than Booth's jet-black mane. Apart from these hardly noticeable differences, they could have been twins.

By the end of October, J. W. Boyd was transferred to the Old Capital Prison in Washington. The transfer was ordered by Baker, but signed by Stanton, who, at that point, had no clue about Boyd's potential, other than his purported skill as a telegrapher, which might make him a valuable asset for the NPD.

Baker made a deal with Boyd. If Boyd swore allegiance to the Union and worked as a double agent in the prison, after the war he would be pardoned and awarded land and money in Mexico. Having no other option, and being grateful for the generous offer, Boyd gladly accepted and went diligently to work. But by February of 1865, he became deeply depressed after learning that his wife had finally passed away. He begged Stanton for an early pardon. He was desperate.

On February 15th, Stanton agreed to an early release from prison, but not from duty. Boyd was still under the control of the NPD. His handler was one of Baker's special detectives. Though Boyd was still far from home, his spirits were raised by the prospect of a future with his family. He had no idea that in reality, he was waiting in the wings as a stunt double for Booth.

For months, Boyd's missions took him across enemy lines and back, while the special agents who were escorting him waited for the word to pull the trigger, so Booth would be brought to justice. But after Lincoln's murder, things had gotten a bit more complicated.

Thanks to Fletcher's mistaken identification, Herold was already in Baker's custody, not on the run with Booth as the country had been told. Baker's detectives seized him at his sister's house the day after Lincoln was shot. With Herold under lock and key in the Old Capital Prison and Boyd in the hands of the NPD, Baker had his cast of understudies assembled. Now all he had to do was stage the final scene.

By Easter dinner, Baker had assembled his elite team for the manhunt. Led by his cousin Lieutenant Luther Baker, the small group, which included James William Boyd, a couple other special detectives, and their guide, David E. Herold, saddled up on Monday, April 17, 1865, in search of the fugitives. Of course, only Luther Baker knew the specific details of the mission.

As the special-op team plunged deeper into Maryland, Captain Boyd grew suspicious about the operation. Though he kept it to himself, he couldn't help but feel he was not so much an agent as a prisoner. His position in the cavalcade was closer to the manacled Herold at the rear than up front with Luther Baker. It's unlikely that Boyd or Herold would have seen any of the numerous "Wanted" posters with photos of Booth and Herold plastered all over every village and town. The Baker unit was tracking Booth over rivers and through the forests and swamps. But at some point – no one knows exactly when – the two understudies began to talk and put two and two together, and eventually they decided to make their move. I suppose they reasoned that if they were going to assume the roles of fugitives-at-large, they might as well start acting like them, or maybe Baker told them straight out, "You have eight hours. Good luck." In any event, at the pre-determined moment, Boyd and Herold took their weapons and horses. By the time the squad decamped the next morning, they were thirty miles away.

Conveniently for Baker, Boyd and Herold we forced to follow Booth and Henson's escape route. It was their only chance of survival. As Baker's detectives tracked them – at a relatively relaxed pace – they discovered various personal items dropped by Booth in transit, including his diary. These belongings would later prove to be crucial pieces of evidence in the identification of John Wilkes Booth. At the barn, Luther Baker and Lieutenant-Colonel Everton Conger, another of Lafayette's special detectives, planted them on the body of Boyd. In reality, these artifacts were purposefully placed there by Booth, before he and Henson boarded the boat across the Rappahannock.

When he and Henson landed on the other side of the river in Virginia, they turned west and made an unobstructed exit to freedom through modern-day West Virginia. When they got to Kentucky, they split up to avoid being recognized. In Warfield, Booth crossed the Big Sandy River and continued traveling southwest for a couple of days, all the while playing the part of a wounded Confederate soldier, of which there were plenty back then. When he made it to Mississippi, Booth knew he was home free. Uncle Sam was waiting with open arms.

Boyd and Herold also made it to Virginia. Unfortunately for them, when they stepped off the ferry they were met by Lieutenants Ruggles and Bainbridge. Former Confederate soldiers, Ruggles and Bainbridge agreed to lead the two men to safety at Richard Garrett's farm. The next day, Baker's crew dragged James William Boyd's body from old Dick's barn.

8

THE HOLOCENE EPOCH

We walked through the east gate of Green Mount Cemetery a little after five. The sun was in our eyes. It was moving fast toward the next morning, forcing the shadows of the old tombstones to slant sharply toward us. It was a beautifully eerie sight.

As we approached Junius's monolith I couldn't help but sense its shadow was a tragic one, fitting for Junius. Shakespeare's tragedies were said to have been his true genius, but that's not why people visited his grave. No, any fame he may have achieved as an actor on this continent has long been overshadowed by his kin's. The star that was once Junius Booth is now as dead as the giant rock on top of his bones. Did he ever really roam the earth?

It's difficult to imagine all the hopes and dreams he once had for himself, his family, his son, the heartfelt tears he shed the moment he held John in his arms for the first time. I suppose one upside to his oblivion is that he never lived to see John fulfill his destiny. There's at least solace in that.

The four of us gathered on the rectangular patch of grass that surrounds the giant obelisk. No tombstone exists for John. That was a major stipulation when the government returned his remains for re-interment back in 1869, four years after he was killed. They didn't want his grave to become a Mecca for radical insurrectionists and Southern sympathizers. Instead, his name is simply inscribed, along with the rest of his brothers and sisters, on Junius's monument. The lack of a proper marker, however, doesn't discourage tourists of a certain persuasion from tossing pennies into the family plot to pay their respects to the assassin.

While the girls and I casually read the various inscriptions along Junius's tombstone, Daniel circled around us and snapped photos. He was trying to capture the perfect light. We didn't last long. The temperature had dropped quite dramatically since we left Bel Air. And there wasn't much to do, apart from watch Daniel take pictures. After a while Monica chimed in.

"I don't understand," she said. "Why don't your friends just dig him up here, and run the tests on his parents or siblings? Why go through all the trouble with the museum and Edwin?"

Daniel paused his photo shoot for a moment.

"They tried to," he said, "back in the mid-nineties, but the court struck them down. It turns out John, or rather the man shot in the barn, isn't even buried in this plot. They actually buried him in some other undisclosed section of the cemetery, to deter vandals and grave robbers. On those grounds, the traditionalists who forced the petition into court argued that any exhumation effort to find John Wilkes Booth would amount to an archeological dig, which would never get approval. Nate Orlowek and his team tried to appeal the ruling, but lost, leaving the only possible alternative to be Booth's vertebrae at the Medical Museum and Edwin in Cambridge."

The girls accepted the explanation, or at least they appeared to, but I could tell their interest in keeping warm was fast eclipsing their interest in the Booths.

"I don't know about you guys," Monica said, finally, "but I'm freezing. Are you gonna be much longer? I could use a warm drink."

Daniel smiled. "No," he said, and turned off his camera. "I think I've gotten enough for one day. What do you say you ladies join us for dinner back at our hotel?"

Monica smiled. "We were wondering when you were going to ask."

"Well, then it's settled."

"You lead the way," she said, with a roll of her fingers.

And that's how we said goodbye to the Booths of Baltimore. Daniel took one more shot of the cemetery, then we all walked briskly to the street and in less than twenty minutes we were at the Plaza Hotel, where the climate was much more hospitable.

We arrived just after sunset. The sky was stunning. St. Paul's Church was aglow with an orange and purple halo above its twin steeples. I checked us in, and then Daniel and I quickly threw our bags in the room and raced downstairs to meet the girls. When we got to the restaurant, they were already sitting in the dining room. It was quite a sight to behold them. Their demeanor had changed remarkably with the sunset. They appeared more elegant in darkness. They were now wearing jewelry. They were now proper ladies.

Like two roses they sat next to each other at the end of a long, pink velvet bench that stretched across the back wall of the main dining room. Their legs were hidden beneath a sea of white linen tablecloth. With big glossy smiles that reflected the light of the large crystal chandelier hanging in the center of the room, they indicated our chairs were waiting for us. We slipped into them comfortably, willingly, our backs exposed to the elements.

From there, the evening passed in a swirling carousel of meats and fish and lambrusco. With each passing course, I felt more and more like a wealthy passenger on a ship across the Atlantic. We ate and drank for hours. The more the wine went around, the more our conversation blossomed into high-minded existentialism. Daniel and Monica did most of the talking at first, while Francesca and I remained mostly quiet in the background, much as it had been all day. I didn't want to impede on or interfere, in any way, with Daniel's path to glory.

I recall one exchange, in particular, quite vividly. It culminated with a surprisingly profound revelation from Daniel that had a marked effect on the table. Around the time our entrees arrived, Monica, who had been pressing Daniel on his theories all evening, asked him point blank, "Why is it so important whether or not Booth got away?"

At first, it looked like she got him. Daniel put his fork down and inhaled deeply through his nose, then exhaled just as deeply.

By this point more people had filtered into the dining room and the volume had increased substantially. He took his time answering.

"I suppose," he said, finally, and I paraphrase a little, "because I think about history, like I think about math or science. We can probably all agree that each of these disciplines is very important to us as a civilization. They tell us about a multitude of things. They help us solve problems. They inform us about our past, where we come from, and so on. They help us discover our universe. They might even save the human race. But what they each have in common is the need to be fundamentally established, and purely rooted in fact and truth. We as a society, as a civilization, cannot really move forward unless we have the truth. Otherwise, the equation just doesn't add up. That's the world we live in now."

He paused to take a slug of wine, then continued, pausing often to carefully choose his words.

"Just like until Einstein everyone just accepted every particle of Newton's laws, for over two hundred years, just as important as it is to know the theory of relativity, it's important to know about Alexander, and Caesar, and Napoleon, and even more importantly, as Americans, to know the truth about Lincoln. And if the truth about his killer is flawed, our understanding of the whole episode is built on false assumptions. Even if it seems to make sense, how do you really know, for sure? One of the most pivotal periods in our nation's history. We're still living with the effects of the Civil War and the inadequate reforms of Reconstruction today, the actions of commanders and politicians that have been buried in oblivion, continued racial injustice, the gridlock in Washington. But unlike so much of history that has been lost, in this case we actually have the possibility of getting to the bottom of it."

As soon as Daniel was finished, Monica launched into a rebuttal of his monologue, which quickly evolved into a charged discourse about conspiracy theories, at large, in which Francesca and I quickly found we were not invited to participate.

We looked at each other at one point and smiled. Daniel and Monica, of course, were oblivious to it. Their eyes were now intensely fixed on each other. But though Francesca was much less talkative than her friend, she wasn't any less seductive. After a brief uncomfortable silence, she began to put her own voice to work, and I began to be taken in by her.

It turned out we had plenty to talk about. My first impression of her as a spacey coquette vanished. Though there's no way she could have been over thirty, she had an appealing sophistication and maturity. She spoke incredibly well, for a girl we just plucked from the farm. She took me completely by surprise when she talked at great length about the Quaternary Period and Homo erectus. In tremendous detail she expounded on the effects of the Holocene epoch on northern Africa, in particular ancient Egypt. It was all quite fascinating. She talked as though she had a PhD in archeology. When I finally asked her what she did for a living, I confess, I was more than a little surprised when she told me she was a business consultant.

After a long journey through the Sahara, where I was as lost as the lost tribe of Israel, I learned how she and Monica knew each other. According to Francesca, they both grew up in Bel Air and were close friends throughout their childhood. Now that they had moved to opposite ends of the country, they made a point of visiting their parents, who still lived in the area, at the same time, so they could stay connected. It all sounded perfectly convincing to me. Why would I have any cause to doubt her? Then my turn came.

"So what about you?" she asked, confidentially. "You're very mysterious."

I chuckled at the thought of being mysterious, "That's one way to put it, I suppose."

"Are you married?" she asked, looking at my wedding finger.

I smiled. What else could I do? Frown?

"Not anymore," I answered.

I took a sip of wine and looked over at the bar, where Daniel and Monica had relocated after we had all sufficiently gorged ourselves. I saw Daniel whisper something into her ear that made her laugh heartily. The intense philosophical debate appeared to have taken a recess. They were now loosened up and looked as though they were genuinely enjoying themselves.

"Oh," Francesca said, bringing the focus back to me, "I'm sorry to hear it, unless of course it was a good thing."

"It was complicated. I won't bore you with the details. But yes, ultimately it was a positive decision." And that was that. She let it die there.

Thankfully, I was spared the agony of reliving it all again, the painful divorce from a woman I once loved deeply, the disdain of my only son, how my life had slipped away because of my own self-inflicted illness and stupidity, how I was professionally ruined.

Luckily, I didn't have to explain all that. Instead, Francesca looked at me with sympathetic eyes, not pity, but empathy, and said, "So should we switch to gin, then, or get another bottle of red?" Everything about her presence was soothing. I was relieved and, unusually, at peace.

Shortly after our waiter brought over another bottle of lambrusco, Daniel and Monica returned to the table to tell us they were going to take the truck for a spin. They asked us if we wanted to join them. I thought for sure Francesca would jump at the opportunity. To my astonishment, she declined, opting instead to continue chatting with me.

"Have fun, Doc." Those were Daniel's parting words as he skipped off merrily with Monica. "Don't wait up." But what about Francesca? What was she supposed to do?

"We'll think of something," she reassured me.

This turned out to be another bottle of wine. God knows what we talked about, but with Daniel and Monica out of the picture, our conversation took on a more intimate tone. If I remember correctly, it was over our fourth bottle of lambrusco that Francesca finally decided to call me out.

"You're not really his dad, are you," she said. The room swirled around her.

"No," I told her, "And you're not really a business consultant."

For the life of me, I don't know why I wasn't more suspicious when she confirmed my lucky guess. Perhaps because I never expected her to. I was very drunk by that point and totally hypnotized by her. In hindsight, neither of us reacted with the slightest bit of horror.

"So what do you think about his quest?" she inquired, referring to Daniel.

I remember thinking a long time before answering the question, all the while the room appeared to gradually narrow on Francesca. It felt like I had all the time in the world to answer her. I hadn't been so comfortably drunk in years.

"I had an uncle who used to live in Washington," I'm pretty sure I began by saying. I had told the story many times before. "He was born and raised in Virginia. He went to college with J. Edgar Hoover at George Washington University, as did my uncle's best friend. But after graduation, my uncle's friend followed in the same line of work as Hoover and later became one of his most trusted lieutenants at the FBI, whereas my uncle went ostensibly into another line of work entirely. Us kids were always told he was a successful lawyer, who had founded a very successful law firm. But that's not what's so interesting about him.

"Uncle Tom's true passion in life was shooting. For several years in the nineteen-fifties, we were told, he was the best rifleman in the country. He won several gold medals for the U.S. in the Olympics, that's how good he was, and he was always traveling to these exotic cities and places around the world to shoot. But what struck us kids as odd was that with all of Uncle Tom's connections and skills and abrupt success in law, and given the fact that he was always traveling to mysterious 'shooting events,' how could he not be a secret agent for Hoover?"

Miraculously, Francesca appeared to be awake and attentively listening to my long tangential answer to her question, or maybe that was just my own narcissistic interpretation. In any event, I continued toward my conclusion.

"How could he not have worked for the FBI?" I continued. "There were many other irregularities that backed up our theory. We had it worked out from every angle. In fact, we had it worked out so well we eventually arrived at the conclusion that Hoover had our Uncle Tom killed because he knew too much."

"Maybe he did," Francesca said.

"You're right. Maybe he did. But more likely, he didn't. And all the circumstantial evidence my cousins and I whimsically pieced together was all just fantasy to make ourselves feel like we were more a part of history than we really were. As I've gotten older, I've come to realize that as strange as things appear sometimes, as improbably coordinated as certain phenomena may be, the true phenomenon is usually just coincidence.

"Until I met Daniel," I continued, "I mostly believed that these conspiracy theorists were a bunch of paranoid schizophrenics trying to make sense out of their own fucked-up internal messaging. As far as I'm concerned, the jury's still out on Daniel and all the rest of the gang. But if this test goes through and it turns out Booth got away, I'm not going to turn my back on it. I'm not the Pope. Then again, I don't have the Vatican at stake."

I'm sure I garbled it much worse than that, that night, but somehow it didn't seem to offend her. When the restaurant closed up, I invited her up to the room and, miraculously, she accepted. I remember we went up the elevator blissfully. She held my arm tight, then quite unexpectedly, she kissed me, but that's the last thing I remember from that night.

(DANIEL'S NOTES)
DAVID E. GEORGE

On January 17th, 1903, the Oklahoma Daily Wave ran the following special report:

> David E. George, a wealthy resident of the Oklahoma Territory, who committed suicide here, announced himself on his deathbed to be John Wilkes Booth, the assassin of President Lincoln. He stated that he had successfully eluded the officers after shooting Lincoln and since had remained incognito.
>
> His statement caused a sensation, and an investigation was made. Surgeons examined the body and stated the man to be the age Booth would be at this time, and announced that his leg was broken in the same place and in the same manner as that of Booth after jumping from the President's box at Ford's Theater after the assassination.
>
> George committed suicide in the Grand Avenue Hotel, taking poison. He previously attempted suicide at El Reno. A letter found in his pocket addressed, 'To

Whom It May Concern,' sets aside a former will which he made, although its contents are not known. He was worth about thirty thousand dollars, owning property in El Reno, Oklahoma; in Dallas, Texas; and a lease on six hundred acres in the Indian Territory. He carried $5,000 insurance.

No reason for the suicide is known. George maintained on his death bed to his attendants that he was John Wilkes Booth, and his general appearance closely resembles that of the murderer of Lincoln.

That same day, a retired lawyer by the name of Finis Bates got an urgent telegram at his home in Memphis, Tennessee. The message was short and clear. It expressly requested he travel as soon as possible to Enid to identify the body of David E. George.

Bates wasted no time. He took the first available train, but by the time he arrived at Enid station news of the story had spread, and the depot was a literal mob scene. Reporters, veterans, and ex-confederates from all over the country had made the pilgrimage to see if the rumors were true.

To Bates' surprise, the instant he stepped off the train he was met by a clerk from the Grand Avenue Hotel who warned him that his arrival had been greatly anticipated by everyone in the town. "They're all waiting to hear what you have to say," said the clerk.

By that point the whole town had heard about the letter, one of several found in George's room at the time of his death. It instructed "to whom it may concern" to contact "Mr. Finis L. Bates of Memphis, TN, in the event of death or severe illness. He can attest to my true identity."

"There was a large number of old Federal soldiers in the city who intended to take the body into the streets and burn it, if it should be identified as that of John Wilkes Booth," Bates wrote in his diary.

To avoid such a riot, special arrangements had been made to conduct the identification in private. The hotel clerk instructed Bates to present himself as "Charles O'Connor," a salesman from a furniture house in New York City specializing in feather-top mattresses. This alias would allow Bates to slip secretly into the morgue – which happened to be in the back of William B. Penniman's furniture store on Main Street – and identify the body.

An hour after checking into the Grand Avenue Hotel, Bates, or rather Charles O'Connor, made his way to Penniman's furniture store to view the remains of David E. George.

"On entering the store I saw a number of clerks, all busy," Bates wrote. "At the center desk was a handsome man of thirty-five or forty." This turned out to be Bill Penniman.

After a brief exchange, Penniman told Bates he had some important business to attend to at the moment, but would return shortly. He then invited Bates to sit down, discreetly pointed to a pile of papers on the desk, and exited the room.

"The papers," Bates described later, "were those containing the news of George's suicide, etcetera, as well as photographs taken of him after death. I could only admire this delicate way of furnishing me, unobserved, the means of identifying the body without actually seeing it, if it should not be opportune to do so. The recognition of John was instantaneous."

A few minutes later, Penniman returned.

"So, Mr. Penniman," O'Connor said, "how are you off for feather-top mattresses?"

"As it so happens, I have none in stock," Penniman answered and conveniently invited Bates to view his inventory, all the while continuing the fabricated conversation of prices, grades of mattresses, and furniture, etc. to throw any would-be eavesdroppers off the trail.

Finally, Penniman swiftly led Bates through a tiny discreet side entrance to the morgue. Upon entering the antechamber, Penniman introduced Bates to the man in charge of the body. That man led them through yet another door, deeper inside the building, and ultimately to the room where the corpse lay supine on a table.

"There, in the presence of the attendant and Mr. Penniman," wrote Bates, "cold, stiff and dead I beheld the body of the man who had been called by the people in this community David E. George, my friend John St. Helen, or John Wilkes Booth. After a separation of more than twenty-six years I knew him as instantly as men discern night from day, starlight from moonlight."

(DANIEL'S NOTES)
JOHN ST. HELEN

Today, Enid is an up-and-coming city in northern Oklahoma. With a population of 49,000, it's the ninth largest city in the state. Also known as the "Wheat Capital of the US," Enid boasts numerous sights and attractions that claim to satisfy the demands of even the harshest critic. When in Enid, travel blogs recommend one visit the old giant grain elevators on the east side of town, or check out Leonardo's Discovery Warehouse, should you be scientifically inclined, or need to entertain school age children for any length of time.

Indeed, today Enid is quite civilized. The local gentry eat fish and chips at Callahan's Pub and Grille, then head over to the Symphony to catch the latest concert. But ask any one of them about John Wilkes Booth, and they'll smile and ask you if you've been to Garfield Furniture yet. This historical landmark in the town square is the former site of the Grand Avenue Hotel, where David E. George, at the age of 63, took a lethal dose of strychnine, forever altering the history of John Wilkes Booth.

Enid certainly has changed a lot since George took that poison. For starters, Oklahoma is now a state. Back then, it was more or less Indian Territory, although that was rapidly changing. When the United States bought the territory from Napoleon in the Louisiana Purchase, the land was originally supposed to go to the Native Americans who had been displaced by the early settlers. But during the Civil War, the Five Civilized Tribes, who predominately occupied Oklahoma at the time—the Cherokee, Choctaw, Muscogee, Chickasaw, and Seminole—fought on behalf of the Confederacy. In fact, Confederate Brigadier General Stand Watie, of the Cherokee nation, was the last commander in the Confederacy to surrender in the Civil War on June 23, 1865.

It's difficult to gauge the ultimate impact of General Watie's career as a soldier on his tribe and the Native American population as a whole, but it was not positive. After the war, the population of the Five Civilized Tribes was chopped in half, and the Sooner State, as we know it today, was founded on November 16, 1907. That same year, the Historical Publishing Co. of Memphis, Tennessee, published the first edition of "The Escape and Suicide of John Wilkes Booth: or The First True Account of Lincoln's Assassination Containing A Complete Confession By Booth Many Years After The Crime," written "for the correction of history" by none other than Finis L. Bates.

The publisher claimed the contents of the book revealed, in full detail, "the plans, plots and intrigue of the conspirators, and the treachery of Andrew Johnson, then Vice-President of the United States." Bates dedicated the book to the "Armies and Navies of the late Civil War, fought between the States of North America, from 1861 to 1865."

"It is a fact that Booth was not killed," Bates began, right out of the stable, "but made good his escape by the assistance of some of the officers of the Federal Army and government of the United States…traitors to President Lincoln."

Bates fancifully described first meeting John Wilkes Booth in the spring of 1872, as Bates was "entering the threshold of manhood." At the time, Bates was a lawyer in his teens residing in Grandberry, Texas, near the Bosque Mountains. Among his first clients was a merchant who had been indicted by the Federal Court in Tyler, Texas, for selling tobacco and whiskey at his former place of residence in Glenrose Mills, twenty miles southwest of Grandberry. The defendant evidently had failed to obtain the proper license for such a business. The violation was punishable as a misdemeanor by fine or imprisonment.

Located on the Bosque River, Glenrose Mills consisted of little more than a water-powered mill and some surrounding log cabins. Out of one of these log cabins, Bates' client had run his tobacco and whiskey trade, before relocating to Grandberry. After he moved, the cabin was occupied by a man known as John St. Helen, who operated a similar business.

Bates' client had been arrested by the U.S. marshal, but had been given bond to appear in Tyler, Texas, to answer the Federal charge. Upon learning that St. Helen was running a similar operation, Bates traveled to Glenrose Mills and asked him if he would testify in Federal Court on behalf of the defendant. At this point, perhaps due to his lack of experience as a lawyer, Bates got sucked into the vortex of John Wilkes Booth.

According to Bates, St. Helen said he needed some time to think about the proposition. Bates respected this wish and returned to Grandberry. A few days later, St. Helen walked into Bates' law office and requested to be heard in a private conference room. Bates obliged. Upon shutting the door, St. Helen expressed his desire to retain Bates as his attorney, representing him in all legal matters. After they both agreed to a reasonable retainer fee, St. Helen got down to business.

"Now, that I have employed you and paid your retainer fee," St. Helen told Bates, "you, as my lawyer, will and must keep secret such matters as I shall confide in you touching my legal interest and personal safety, and the prevention of my prosecution by the courts for the matters we are now considering or that might hereafter arise in consequence of your present employment."

"I understand," said Bates.

"Well, then," St. Helen continued, "I say to you, as my attorney, that my true name is not John St. Helen, as you know me and suppose me to be, and for this reason I cannot afford to go to Tyler before the Federal Court, in fear that my

true identity be discovered…the risk would be too great for me to take, and you will now understand why I have retained you as my counsel."

Bates wrote that St. Helen asked him to take his client, the merchant, to Federal Court in Tyler and get him clear of his charge, using Bates' best judgment on behalf of both clients' protection. For this service, St. Helen paid Bates a fee and all costs involving the trial and trip to Tyler. Bates succeeded in all particulars of the mission, and so began their friendship.

Toward the end of June, a few months after the trial in Tyler, St. Helen visited Bates' office and invited him to a Fourth of July barbecue at his property at Glenrose Mills, where the pair had first met. Bates accepted the invitation and arrived on the appointed day and was met by St. Helen, the master of ceremonies. It seems that the barbecue resembled more of a royal reception than a picnic.

"With his servants in waiting all were attentive," Bates wrote of his impressions, "while St. Helen entertained us with lavish hand in princely welcome in that manner peculiarly his own."

Bates went on to describe St. Helen, the performer: "In short, eloquent and timely speech, he completely captivated the crowd by his pre-eminent superiority. His complete knowledge of elocution, ease and grace of person, together with his chaste and eloquent diction, seemed to be nature's gift, rather than studied effort."

Throughout the course of the afternoon it became clear that the master of ceremonies was truly an orator of the highest class, but who could he be? Where did he come from? And why, of all places, was he in Glenrose Mills? These were the questions that overcame Bates that afternoon. It took him many years to discover the answers, at which point more questions emerged.

By fall of the same year, St. Helen moved from Glenrose Mills to Grandberry and, at all times, appeared to have more money than someone in his line of work should. He was a man of leisure who outwardly took very little interest in his business affairs. He spent much of his time in Grandberry in Bates' office, reading or entertaining the young lawyer after business hours.

"In our idle moments," Bates observed, "his favorite occupation was reading Shakespeare's plays, or rather reciting them as he alone could do. And his special preference seemed to be that of Richard III."

Bates described how, on more than one occasion, he took lessons in elocution from St. Helen. The more time they spent together, the more Bates' interest in the true identity of this out-of-place drifter grew. But nothing could have prepared Bates for the bombshell St. Helen would drop on him years later.

Approximately five years after they met, St. Helen became gravely ill. "Emaciated, sick and weak," Bates recalled, "he took to his bed, confined in the back room of his store, where I and others, with the aid of a physician, gave him such attentions as his condition required."

Then one night around 10 o'clock, the doctor told Bates that St. Helen was dying and that the invalid's last request was to speak with Bates alone. Bates obeyed and arrived at his friend's bedside. St. Helen was weak. He could only faintly speak in broken words and sentences. Bates asked of what service he could be, then placed his ear close to St. Helen's mouth for a response.

"I am dying," St. Helen confessed. "My name is John Wilkes Booth, and I am the assassin of President Lincoln. Get the picture of myself from under the pillow. I leave it with you for my future identification. Notify my brother Edwin Booth, of New York City."

St. Helen then closed his eyes and fell fast asleep. Before calling for the porter, Bates reached under St. Helen's pillow and uncovered the picture, a small tintype taken shortly before he took ill. Shocked and bewildered, Bates slipped the picture into his coat pocket. St. Helen would surely be dead by morning and what then, Bates thought.

Much to the surprise of everyone, however, St. Helen lived through the night, and within a few days he was up and walking again. All who witnessed the miraculous recovery were stunned, but none more than Bates a week or so later when he dropped by St. Helen's apartment and discovered that the man who called himself Booth had vanished without a trace. It would be over two decades before Bates would see him again, but by then St. Helen would truly be dead. His corpse, last known as David E. George, now known as the mummy, is still at large....

IDES OF MARCH

I awoke the next morning not entirely sure of where I was. When my eyelids found the strength to stay open, the scenery vaguely matched my memory of our hotel room, but it took some time to put it together. I was still terribly drunk. My muscles were unusually sore and my mouth was cracking with dryness.

Lying numb on my side, I tried to recall the details of the previous evening, but so much had been blacked out. How did I get into the bed? How did I get into the room? I had no memory of it. What happened after we got out of the elevator? Was Francesca with me? Where was Daniel?

When I rolled over, Francesca was not in bed next to me. But in the adjacent bed, Daniel was sound asleep. I was relieved to see him in one piece. I'll never forget the expression on his face. It was so stern, yet so earnest, as if, even in his deepest slumber he was dreaming of Booth.

Meanwhile, I painfully went about resurrecting myself. I sat up and rubbed my face. I was still dressed in my clothes from the night before, and every last inch of me ached. What the hell happened last night, I wondered, teetering on the edge of consciousness.

Everything was in slow motion, until I put my glasses on and caught sight of the clock, then all at once time accelerated.

It was late, fifteen minutes past checkout. I remembered Daniel had an appointment with the museum director in less than forty-five minutes and the car ride alone was over an hour. I sprung up and tried to get him out of bed, but he was in bad shape.

I turned on the television. I opened the windows. I tried talking to him. I told him we were late, that he would miss his appointments. But at the depths of his hangover, Daniel seemed willing to give it all up.

"We can push it back," he moaned incoherently from under his pillow. He sounded like he was in agony.

I took a quick shower, hoping he'd get moving in the meantime, but when I returned, he was in the same position with the pillow over his head. After I packed up, I told him I was going downstairs to check out, and that he needed to meet me in the lobby in ten minutes, before housekeeping kicked him out. I hated playing the tough guy, but I didn't know what else to do.

Miraculously, it worked. Ten minutes after I walked out of the room, Daniel stepped out of the elevator into the lobby wearing his shades and carrying his suitcase. Walking toward me through a forest of gray-hairs, he appeared to morph into a vision of a naïve young man, dangerously exploring an old man's world. Looking back, it's startling just how prescient this moment really was.

"Are we all set?" he asked softly, when he approached me at the front desk.

"Everything's all settled," I told him.

"What about the car?" he asked.

"The valet's bringing it round now."

"Great," he said with a sigh of relief. "We can get coffee on the road. By the way," he added, "thanks."

"You're welcome," I said.

Within seconds the valet drove the car up and handed me the keys, and Daniel and I raced to the museum.

We spoke very little on the ride. Daniel was in no mood for conversation. For most of the trip, he silently stared out the window. I can only imagine what he must have been thinking behind his dark sunglasses. I wasn't privy to the intimate details of his experience the night before, but perhaps for the first time in months, Daniel's mind may have been consumed by something other than Booth, at least for a few moments anyhow.

At a minute before 12:30 pm, we pulled up outside the National Museum of Health and Medicine. The drive was surprisingly short. The most difficult part of it all was locating the actual building itself, after the GPS told us we had arrived at our destination. It's tucked away in an unusual spot for a museum. Then again, this particular museum is an unusual cultural institution.

Founded as the Army Medical Museum in 1862 by Surgeon General William Hammond, its original mission, according to the official government charter, was to document injuries, disease, and deaths due to war and armed combat. In reality, however, it was created by the War Department to oversee the nation's medical system during the Civil War. That's why on the night President Lincoln was shot, Army Medical Museum staff were among the first officials to be contacted. It's why museum director, and Edwin Stanton protégé, Dr. Joseph K. Barnes supervised Lincoln's autopsy. It's also how the War Department became directly involved in the identification and autopsy of John Wilkes Booth. The whole affair was orchestrated and certified by Dr. Barnes.

Onboard Stanton's warship in the Washington Navy Yard, less than two weeks after the president was killed, Barnes declared to the military commission, "as sure as the earth revolves around the sun, this is the body of John Wilkes Booth." Barnes then proudly claimed the third, fourth, and fifth cervical vertebrae of the corpse, which were removed in order to dislodge the bullet fired from Boston Corbett's gun, and deposited them into the Army Medical Museum's vault of treasures.

Though the museum's mission, like its name, has evolved over the years, the institution still falls under the authority of the Department of Defense. The Army, not the Smithsonian, signs its paychecks. That's why, today, the bone specimens of "John Wilkes Booth" are held at the National Museum of Health and Medicine's headquarters, discreetly located on the campus of the U.S. Army's Forest Glen Annex in Silver Spring, Maryland. To get to the museum, you first must drive through a military checkpoint. Once you get past that hurdle, you have to navigate your way through a maze of military barracks, following very confusing signs that thwart you at every turn. It's almost as if they're purposely trying to mislead you.

On the afternoon of our visit, the journey was quite nerve-wracking. With Daniel over a half-hour late for his interview, the last thing we needed was to be hunting around for a hidden museum. But eventually we spied a large cement building through a thin, man-made forest. When we finally confirmed it was the right place, Daniel jumped out of the car and raced down a long blockaded sidewalk that led down a glade to the main entrance. As I followed, I noticed a stunning array of clouds that expanded across the sky from behind the mysterious building. Reminiscent of a bomb shelter, the massive post-modern puzzle of warped cubes and bulletproof glass looked as though a sprawling bushel of cotton was growing out of it.

When I walked through the giant glass doors, Daniel was sitting on a bench in the main lobby next to the front desk, vacantly staring off into space. Looking around, I was surprised by how dead it was. We seemed to be the only ones in the museum.

"Are you gonna get in to see her?" I asked.

Maybe it was the light, more likely it was the alcohol, but he did not look good. His face looked paler than I remembered in the car. He suddenly appeared weak and vulnerable, as if he knew he really fucked up and now was at the mercy of the universe.

"Yes," he answered. "They told me to wait here. She just stepped into another meeting, but is expecting me, they say."

Elizabeth Colburn was her name. She's the head curator of the museum's Anatomical collection. Daniel had never met her in person before, but had spoken to her over the phone and emailed her several times over the course of many months, he said, and led me to believe that she was a charming woman who had a soft spot for him.

"You want any water?" I asked.

"I'm all right," he said. "I'm just trying to focus. I can't seem to think straight."

"You'll pull it together," I told him glibly.

While he waited and sweated it out, I casually strolled through the halls. The exhibits were amusing. There were pickled brains and other various organs preserved in formaldehyde everywhere you turned and a plethora of skeletons, but I was particularly struck by the historic exhibits displaying the numerous medical advancements over the last hundred and fifty years. It's refreshing to be reminded just how far medicine has come in such a short period of time.

It's startling enough to think about the advancements since I was in medical school, but to imagine the types of tools they used during the Civil War is astonishing. The medical kits were archaic. They were practically using hacksaws at a time when anesthesia was still a budding development. Cocaine and opium were the most popular drugs of the day. Compare that with 3-D CT scans, and beta-blockers, and the infinite variety of instruments we have today. The progress is truly amazing.

After roaming through the halls for a good half-hour or so, I casually turned a corner, past Walter Reed's legendary microscope, and saw Daniel standing down the hall, next to the same bench in the lobby, talking to a thin, fairly attractive brunette, who I assumed was Elizabeth Colburn, and an older, heavy-set man in a gray suit.

The old man turned and glanced at me. His face, at once, was arresting. The instant he saw me through his large thick glasses, his jowls pinched into a sneer. The woman I suspected was Ms. Colburn gave me a much softer, but equally unsettling scan as well. Then they smoothly returned their eyes back to Daniel, who appeared quite distressed.

His body language was more animated than usual, and his mouth was moving uncharacteristically fast. In contrast, his interviewers seemed as silent and constrained as priests. When I arrived on the scene, Daniel interrupted the conversation and broke the news to me.

"It's off," he said.

I paused.

"What do you mean, 'it's off?' " I asked.

It was then that I was formerly introduced to Ms. Colburn and Mr. Richard Chandler, who told me he was a senior director of special operations for the Defense Department.

"As I was just telling Mr. Boland," said Chandler, with no more emotion than a rock, "this morning the Defense Department received classified information regarding a potential terror threat here at the museum. As a result, all research relating to the Booth testing has been suspended, indefinitely."

"Which means we won't be able to go through with the exhumation," Daniel added.

"Wait a minute," I said. "I'm confused. Has Congressman Christopher been told about this?"

"I notified his staff earlier this morning and spoke to him personally on the phone just now," Ms. Colburn said. "I'm afraid it's quite serious."

Ms. Colburn was well put together. Though significantly younger than her male counterpart, it was impossible to tell her age. She could have been in her late thirties, forties, maybe even fifty. She wore thin bifocals and her hair in a bun. And over a tight-fitting, navy-blue skirt-suit, she had on a white pearl necklace.

"Well," I said, "is there anything more you can tell us?"

"At this point, I'm afraid not," said Chandler, curtly.

After an awkward silence, Daniel began to shake his head.

"It doesn't make sense," he said. "It just doesn't make sense."

Chandler nodded compassionately and said, "I'm sorry to be the one to break it to you."

Then, as if on cue, the fluttering sound of a telephone twittered out from behind the vacant front desk. It may have been my imagination, but I believe the ring prompted an awkward moment between Chandler and Colburn.

"Now if there isn't anything else I can do for you today," Chandler continued between rings, "I believe that's for me."

"Of course," I said. "Please don't let us get in the way. We appreciate your taking the time to speak with us."

But Chandler didn't hear a word I said. Before I finished my first sentence, he vanished behind the front desk. His sudden absence cast a gloomy shadow over the gallery, leaving Ms. Colburn. Notwithstanding, she attempted to soften the blow.

"I'm so sorry to make you come all the way down here for nothing," she said apologetically. "When this is all resolved, I would be happy to speak with you again, and help you in any way I can."

"Thank you," said Daniel, choking back tears. The loss was too painful to bear. "I appreciate it. I just really can't believe this. Yesterday, everything was fine."

Ms. Colburn stood in silence for a moment, and then suddenly stepped toward us.

"You haven't read the newspaper today, have you?" she said, lowering her voice.

We were both taken aback by her abrupt informality.

"Well, no," I confessed.

"They might give you some more insight," she said confidentially, before briskly turning and disappearing, herself, without another word.

12

THE LINCOLN MONUMENT

Seconds after we walked outside, Daniel turned and violently threw up in a nearby bush. In less than five minutes our lives had been turned upside down, but at that point, we didn't know the half of it.

As soon as we got in the car, we followed Ms. Colburn's advice and immediately googled the Baltimore *Sun*. It took seconds for my heart to stop.

"MURDER IN BOOTH'S HOUSE," ran the headline on the *Sun* homepage, "Board Member of Tudor Hall Found Dead in Former Booth Living Room."

As hair-raising as the headline was, the story got worse and worse with each subsequent paragraph. I don't think I ever read a story so carefully in my life.

BEL AIR, Md. – At police headquarters here late Thursday night, local law enforcement officials held an impromptu press conference to confirm the death of 66-year-old Joan Stevens. Her body was discovered earlier that evening inside Tudor Hall, the birthplace of presidential assassin John Wilkes Booth. Over the course of the twenty-five minute press conference, authorities also announced the death was a homicide.

"Mrs. Stevens was savagely murdered in cold blood," said Captain Reginald Thompson of the Bel Air Police Department. "Her throat was cut with a knife and she was left to bleed to death."

Stevens' body was found shortly before 6 p.m. by Tudor Hall Society president Peggy Landruff, who stopped by the former Booth house to tend to some administrative duties.

Nothing was out of the ordinary, Landruff said, until she entered the former Booth living room and saw Stevens lying in a pool of blood. "I screamed and immediately ran out of the building," she said. "It was the most terrible sight I've ever seen."

A retired history professor and mother of three, Stevens served on the executive board and was the historian of the Tudor Hall Society for over a decade.

"It's the single most tragic chapter in the history of Tudor Hall," said Shirley Dawson, the Society's secretary of the board. "Joan was truly synonymous with Tudor Hall. She will be sadly missed."

Steven's husband Fred Stevens attended the press conference with family and friends. Speaking to reporters, he repeatedly broke down in tears.

"I just don't understand why anyone would do this" he said. "It doesn't make any sense."

So far, police have yet to identify any suspects. At the time this paper went to press, authorities were actively searching for the missing vehicle Stevens used to drive to the scene of the crime. It's been identified as a black, 2011, Ford F-150 pick-up truck.

"We have reason to believe that whoever killed Mrs. Stevens drove off with her vehicle," said Captain Thompson. "Locating it as quickly as possible, before it is tampered with, is our number one priority right now."

I finished reading the story and looked at Daniel. He was transfixed. I could feel his blood pressure rising.

"Jesus Christ," he said after he finished. "It just gets worse and worse. I need to call Nate."

"You're not going to tell him about the ladies, are you?" I asked.

"No," he said, rubbing the bridge of his nose, "I just need to speak with him and find out if he knows anything, see if he's talked with anyone else from the team. Maybe they know something we don't."

Daniel attempted to call Nate and the rest of the team, but no one picked up the phone. With each message he left, he became increasingly frustrated. The futility of all his efforts, all he had invested physically and emotionally, was hitting him square in the gut. Fear and panic were written all over his face.

"How come nobody's picking up?" he demanded at one point. "Where is everybody?"

Finally, after what must have been a dozen calls, someone answered. The voice was unmistakable. Though Daniel had his phone pressed tightly to his ear, there was no way to contain Peter Ramsey's voice from booming out of the speaker. He's a very loud man.

Peter Ramsey could probably best be described as a rugged cowboy, well past his prime. He has a giant beer gut, which he throws around unapologetically, and a thick rusty beard and mustache to match. He also has unusually hyperactive eyes. They dart about erratically, as if he's constantly on the lookout for a sniper, which may just be a product of his trade. Peter's specialty, you see, is finding things and people. He's what you call a "skip tracer," or private eye.

I was always told that, by day, Peter worked covertly for some unknown law firm tracking down information and people, and on the side, he moonlighted for the Booth escape team. I have no idea how Peter fared at his day job, but for the escape researchers, at least, he performed his task incredibly well. Since he began working for them, well over a decade ago, he uncovered countless pieces of evidence backing up their case. He's the one who tracked down one of the original documents implicating Lincoln in the meat-for-cotton scandal, which ultimately brought Congressman Christopher to the table.

No one ever knew how or why Peter did what he did. He was always very mysterious. No one knew where he was born, or where he lived, or if he had a family, or anything like that. You never called Peter. He always called you, and seemingly at the most random times. At three in the morning you'd get an urgent call from him about some odd thing or another and he'd expect you to meet him right away to talk about it. He also had an uncanny ability to be anywhere in the country in thirty minutes or less. He was truly an enigma.

Daniel once told me about the first time he met Peter. They emailed back and forth for days to find a time and place to meet in person for an interview. Then a couple days later, Peter calls him up out of the blue and tells him it can't wait. They have to meet that night. It's very important, but nobody can know about it.

At that point, Daniel didn't know Peter at all, so he followed his directions and showed up at the appointed restaurant at the exact minute Peter requested. An hour later, Peter showed up, but instead of joining Daniel right away at the table, he just stood by the front door and talked to the waiters, then went over to the bar and started quietly talking to the bartender, then went to the bathroom and came back and continued his conversation with the bartender again. God knows what they were talking about. When Peter finally sat down with Daniel, he didn't apologize. He hardly even spoke to him, Daniel said. Instead, he asked the waitress for a Jack and Coke then placed a huge order, dessert and all, then picked-up and left the restaurant before the appetizers even came, sticking Daniel with the bill. After that, Daniel didn't hear a word from him for months. That's the type of guy Peter was. But at the museum that afternoon, his crude Southern twang was a soothing voice of reason to Daniel.

"Look," Daniel said over the phone, "I can't go into all the details right now. Can you meet up with us later tonight?"

Peter responded at great length. Exactly what he said, I can't say. During the muffled conversation I scoured the internet for more information on the story. Somewhere along the line I heard Daniel tell him we were staying at the Hay-Adams hotel.

"We should be there within the hour," he said. "Oh, shit," he corrected himself. "Scratch that. I just remembered, I have another interview in an hour at the Mexican Embassy with the Ambassador. I completely forgot. Yeah, it's for this fucking enchilada story. Don't ask."

Peter may not have asked, but he sure blabbed on. All the while, Daniel patiently listened, interjecting with only the occasional "yup" or "right," to let him know he was still on the line.

"Six o'clock is perfect," Daniel said finally. "Meet us in the restaurant then. We'll be hungry. Alright then," he said after another brief pause, "we'll see you then."

Daniel hung up and exhaled a large, "whew." As much of a loose cannon as Peter was, I think Daniel sincerely believed he was the exact type of person we needed to speak to about our current situation.

Unlike our trip to the museum, on the ride to the Embassy Daniel was extremely talkative and energized. Over and over, he bounced questions off me, trying to piece together the events of the previous evening. The aloof and distant Daniel from the previous day had all but disappeared. Instead, in his place was a fragile and needy young man who was looking to me in this crisis to reassure him everything was going to be fine.

It made me think about my son Alex and wonder how he was doing. The only thing I knew about him at that point was that he was a senior at Cal Tech. Beyond that, I was a perfect stranger now. Is this what it might have been like with him, I thought to myself? Shuttling him from one emergency to another? What is it about youth that makes us all so stupid? Might Alex have miraculously learned from his old man's mistakes? Might that have been the only silver lining?

I hoped, silently, for Alex while I hoped for Daniel out loud. He was in a heap of trouble, but at that point, he didn't know the half of it. There were still so many unanswered questions. For instance, neither of us could remember exactly how we got back to our hotel room the previous night. An entire piece of our collective memory seemed to have been deleted.

"You think we were drugged?" Daniel asked.

"It's possible," I told him. I couldn't remember the last time I felt as bad as I did that morning.

"It just doesn't make sense otherwise," he said.

The more we talked about the possibility of being framed, the more the conversation, logically, turned toward indulging various theories that might explain our predicament.

"If this doesn't prove there's a larger conspiracy behind all of this," Daniel said, "I don't know what does."

I tried to steer us away from going down the conspiracy theory road.

"I don't think it's a good idea to make any assumptions, right now," I told him. "Before we start jumping to conclusions, it's critical that everything be rooted in fact. There could be a thousand different explanations for this confluence of events. At this point, we can't rule out the possibility that this all might be a random coincidence."

"You have got to be kidding me," he said. "You can actually sit there and tell me that with a straight face? No, you are actually willing to believe all the shit that you believe, and accept all the truths you hold to be self evident, and yet you can't look at what's right in front of your face right now and accept the truth. It's baffling."

He had a point. Many of the things human beings accept as fact to construct their realities and worldviews are, indeed, quite irrational. I admit, I was in denial. I was in shock. As we turned off the rotary onto Pennsylvania Avenue, nothing felt real to me, not even Washington. What were all these allusions in front of me? What was the truth behind them? Was everything a lie? Could nothing be trusted?

In a blur of all these thoughts, I suddenly found myself idling in front of the Mexican Embassy. It's just down the avenue from the White House, across from the International Monetary Fund. Sandwiched between what appeared to be two giant office buildings, I thought it was a parking garage. If it wasn't for the Mexican flag out front, I'd still have my doubts, but Daniel assured me it was the right place. Before we parted, I asked him if he wanted me to swing back and pick him up after I checked into the hotel.

"No, don't worry about it," he said. "The hotel's right around the corner. The walk will help clear my mind."

And that's how we parted. The second Daniel entered the building, I exhaled a deep breath. It was surprisingly euphoric. At last, I felt I could breathe again. At last, I could let my guard down. I no longer had to hold up a composed exterior. I sat there and indulged the feeling for several minutes, hoping it would ground me, hoping it would set me straight again, but that didn't happen. My mind continued to race.

All I could think was, how did I get involved in this? How did my life get intertwined with this heinous assassin? Was this really my destiny? To play a menial role in a far-fetched conspiracy that may or may not have happened a hundred and fifty years ago, that might still exist today? Was I going to be another victim?

Finally, I decided to turn it all off. I impulsively put my foot on the gas and rounded the first corner I came to. But in just a few short blocks, I was forced to pull over. As I turned onto the Mall, I began sweating and breathing hard. Then tears started streaming down my face. I was having a panic attack. I recognized the symptoms immediately. Since the divorce I had suffered a few of them. I knew there was nothing I could do about it, other than ride it out. After I calmed down a bit, I couldn't help but laugh to think how depressing it would have been if the police pulled up then and there, in full force, and threw me down on the mall and hauled me off to jail with tears bursting from my eyes.

Eventually I pulled myself together and looked out at my surroundings. The view was arresting. The Reflecting Pool, the cherry blossoms, the ghost of Lincoln down the way, gazing out of his house at me. I couldn't see him, but knew he could see me. All of it took me back to the last time I was in Washington, many years ago.

Alex must have been around ten. He was still interested in doing things with his parents. We climbed to the top of the Washington Monument, all three of us. About half way up, Alex challenged me to a race. I accepted and we both dashed to the top, 897 steps. He beat me, of course. When I arrived, huffing and puffing, he laughed and said, "Dad, will we be best friends forever?"

"Of course we will," I told him, choking back tears.

I hugged him and pointed out the White House down below, and a few minutes later Ellen caught up with us. She took the last step and I'll never forget the way she looked. She exhaled a giant breath of relief and smiled, and the way the sunlight hit her strawberry blonde hair and ivy-colored eyes made me weep inside. That smile, I remember it so clearly, the smile that through the years I turned into a tragic frown. She was so patient. All those years she stood by me, through medical school, during the start of my practice, raising our son, everything. I took her for granted. It's the single biggest regret of my life.

It cut me deeply to sit there helplessly like that and think back at those days, not that they were perfect, by any means. No, by that time the alcohol had a firm grip on my soul. By that time, I was a ticking time bomb, but at least there was a chance to avoid calamity. Back then I still had hope that everything might miraculously sort itself out, that I'd wake up one morning and it would all be just a dream, the women, the booze, the lies, and Ellen and I could go back to the way things used to be when we first met in Mitchel Square. Things could have been different.

Instead, I sat alone in my car, a disgraced husband, a disgraced father, a disgraced human being. For a brief moment I thought about picking up my phone and pouring my guts out to them. Much to the relief of everyone involved, I quickly came to my senses, opting instead to sit there in silence, staring out into space, the way Lincoln was said to have done during the bleakest hours of the Civil War. Well, there he sat now in his stone shrine, too enlightened, thankfully, to pass any judgment on me.

I'm not exactly sure how long I stayed there like that. On that afternoon, time passed backward and forward and backward again until, at last, George Washington's giant edifice had disappeared and I was all in, sitting across the table from Daniel and Peter at the Hay-Adams. Food never tasted so good.

After lobster-tail and lamb-chops, the evening continued in the hotel bar. It's supposedly the place for Washington socialites to be seen, and not heard, a decadent speak-easy, where lobbyists and businessmen of every walk of life mingle with political intermediaries beneath the imagery of Washington, Jefferson, and St. John hovering in the background. Luckily, no one was in the place when we took over the booth in the back, because at that point, we still had a lot to discuss.

When the waitress brought over the drinks, Peter obsessed over his. He asked her for more sugar, and salt, and Worcestershire sauce, and God knows what else. It turned my stomach to watch him pinching and stirring and dabbing his pinky in his glass and picking his ear, but Daniel seemed to ignore it entirely.

"So what do you think?" he asked, after Peter took the first sip of his Lynchburg lemonade. "Should we go to the police?"

Peter swished and gargled and shook his head and then painfully swallowed, then answered, "Of course not," with a strained expression on his face.

"But isn't it better to come forward and tell them what we know early to avoid suspicion?" Daniel asked. "I mean, if we wait, doesn't it make us look more guilty?"

"Not necessarily," Peter said. "Any reasonable judge would totally understand why you would have been reluctant to come forward. Besides, at this point, I can't see how they could tie you to the case. You said you didn't leave a paper trail. No emails or texts or anything, right?"

"Right. Just the phone call to Tudor Hall the day before to confirm our appointment, but I called on a private line. The question is did she write my name down anywhere?"

"If she did, you'd know by now. You'd already be in for questioning."

"But then there's also the question of the truck. My prints are all over it!"

"Calm down, calm down," Peter said. "Even if they do find the truck, which might never happen, they're gonna run it for prints, right? Well, I'm assuming the ladies don't want to get caught either, right? Who's to say they didn't wipe it down? In fact, I'm ninety-nine per cent positive they wiped it down. So I would definitely not go out on a limb at this point, no."

As shocked as I was to find myself agreeing with Peter, I was wishfully clinging to his logic.

"Even if they do discover your prints," he added, "how are they going to link them to you? The authorities are going to match them against prints with criminal records. No one saw you, right?"

"No one except the ladies," Daniel said. "We certainly didn't see Joan Stevens."

"Well, that's good. It means no arrows will point to you. And in the worst-case scenario, let's say you were actually set up, that there's some giant political cabal out to get you. Well, then you're fucked anyway. The best thing you can do now is defend yourself. If I were you, I would preemptively write a story for your paper about the whole Goddamn thing. Head the whole thing off before they get to you. "

"Mention the women and all?" Daniel asked.

"No, not the women," said Peter. "Leave them out of it. But write about the terrorist threat, and the museum stalling, again. What are they afraid of? That's the story, in my opinion."

Peter hooked him. I could see Daniel laboriously assembling the jigsaw puzzle in his mind. The muse had struck, and soon he ordered another drink, and another, and another, until yet another night faded into morning. But as groggy as we may have been at day-break, the muse's words had not lost any of their potency. They were still fresh in Daniel's eye.

The last leg of our trip was the Booth Escape Route tour, and Daniel made good use of it. The bus tour was the perfect vehicle for his exposé. As we barnstormed the countryside from Ford's Theater to Doctor Mudd's house, and from Port Tobacco to the former site of Richard Garrett's barn, Daniel furiously scribbled away in his notepad. The instant he filled one page, he dramatically flipped to the next. In between pages, he interviewed our tour guides and fellow passengers. He was overcome with newfound inspiration. He jotted and scratched, then jotted some more again, then tore, before jotting again. Then when he got back to the hotel, he hammered and clacked into his computer.

This is how the rest of our trip went. And the more he banged on his keyboard, the more our night in Baltimore became a distant dream. The peril we faced the day before, at least, temporarily had drifted from his consciousness. His words were going to fix everything.

By the time we returned to New York, Daniel had his story. The Beacon loved it. They ran it as their cover story a couple days later, and it made headlines. The instant it appeared online, the story went viral. Daniel had over twenty interview requests within an hour. From out of his darkest hour, Daniel appeared to be getting everything he dreamed of.

13

BOOTH TESTING HALTED, AGAIN

Why is the Department of Defense Afraid?

By Daniel Boland

Published in print and online by The Brooklyn Beacon

Wednesday, March 20

A month ago, a fringe group of researchers, scientists, and historians got some exciting news. At long last they had been given the green light to perform a DNA test on the remains of Abraham Lincoln's assassin, John Wilkes Booth. The test, they believed, would finally set a one-hundred-and-fifty-year-old mystery straight: was Lincoln's killer actually killed at Garrett's barn the way the history books tell us, or did he escape justice, as some scholars suggest? But last week those hopes were dashed.

On Friday, a special operations director from the Department of Defense (who oversees the operation of the museum) announced that, due to a recent terrorist threat, the Booth testing would be suspended indefinitely, again.

"This is the last straw," said Kathy Beards, a Booth descendant from Philadelphia. "It's an outrage. How much longer can they keep this up?"

If history is any indication, quite a bit longer. For nearly a decade, the National Museum of Health and Medicine (the institution that owns three cervical vertebrae taken from the man shot in the barn) has tirelessly blocked attempts by the group to test the assassin's remains. Disheartened by their futile efforts, escape researchers had all but given up on the idea. But this January when the group won the backing of several members of Congress, including Congressman Calvin A. Christopher of Maryland, the museum was finally forced to take notice.

"For the first time in my lifetime," said Beards, now age 63, "it looked like we were finally going to get to the truth."

Nate Orlowek, the chief researcher and spokesman for the escape team, is not surprised by the DOD's decision. He's been dealing with these kinds of setbacks for forty years, most recently in 1995 when his team attempted to exhume the un-marked grave of the assassin in the Booth family plot at Green Mount Cemetery in Baltimore. After getting approval from the Maryland State's Attorney in Baltimore to go ahead with the exhumation, the president of the cemetery decided to block the proposal at the last minute and force the issue into court.

"The Booth family – the people who own the plot – approved it," said Orlowek recently from his office in Silver Spring, MD. "They were trying to get the body exhumed because they want to know the truth about their own history. And they believe, as we do, that the man killed in the barn was not Booth and they do not want the body of that man buried in their plot."

In the end, the Booth family's wishes were not granted. On the fifth day of the trial – which spanned a week and a half and hours of expert testimony – Baltimore Circuit Court Judge Joseph H. H. Kaplan (a reported Civil War aficionado) decided not to allow the exhumation.

Because "the alleged remains of John Wilkes Booth were buried in an unknown location...and any exhumation would require that the Booth remains be kept out of the grave for an inappropriate minimum of six weeks," His Honor concluded there was no compelling reason for exhumation.

Almost twenty years have passed since Judge Kaplan handed down this decision, but in that time, Orlowek's thinking on the subject, and his determination to get to the truth, has not changed. Nor has it for the Booth family.

Lois Grossman, the great-great grand niece of John Wilkes Booth and the main petitioner in the trial of '95, recently re-affirmed her commitment to the pursuit, despite having reservations about the escape theory.

"I'm not sold on the idea by any stretch of the imagination," said Grossman, "but as a family member, we should be able to know – as best we can – who is buried in the family plot. And if he [her great-great-uncle] escaped, there could be descendants who have a right to know."

In the early 2000s the team came up with a plan to circumvent Green Mount Cemetery. By performing a DNA match test between the cervical artifacts of John Wilkes Booth in the N.M.H.M. collection and the skeleton of his brother, Edwin – who is the only next of kin not buried in Green Mount – the team is certain they can conclusively determine if the specimens were related. If the results are affirmative, it would prove the government got the right man at the barn. If negative, it would prove that John Wilkes Booth escaped.

"There is a long history of successful extraction and analysis of DNA from skeletal remains," said Dr. Erin Kay, the lead forensic scientist for the research team. "DNA persists within the hard tissues for much longer periods of time than in the soft tissues, as conditions within the bone provide some protection against environmental agents that promote DNA degradation."

Dr. Kay added that the DNA extraction procedure would be minimally destructive to the vertebrae. "In most cases," she said, "it requires as little as 0.2 grams of powderized bone material," which would approximately fit on the surface area of a coin.

Sounds convincing enough. So why is the museum stalling? Could something really be there the government doesn't want us to know about? Professor Oswald Kenzie of Georgetown University believes there may be something to that theory.

"The results could have far-reaching consequences," said Kenzie. "If the testing proved that Booth got away, that Lincoln's death, in fact, went unpunished, it could shake the fabric of society."

Professor Jane Harmon disagrees. She teaches sociology at the University of Maryland and is on the board of directors of the Surratt Society, the non-profit museum that runs the conventional Booth Escape Tour, which concludes with Booth's death at the barn. Harmon said, as far as she's concerned, it's not the outcome of the test that's the problem. She's confident the results will back the traditional history she's been studying for over twenty years. What concerns her is how the other side might react if things don't go their way.

"My fear," said Harmon, "is that they go through all of this hoopla and when the answer is finally before them, and they can't deny it anymore, they invent some other reason why it can't be true, because in my experience, true believers will always believe the world is flat and that John Wilkes Booth escaped."

Orlowek, on the other hand, finds Harmon's characterization insulting. He says his team has plenty of evidence to back up its case. "As I said in the exhumation trial in 1995, if a man from Mars were to come down here and he was not to be told which side had had its story believed — the government side or our side — he would look at the government's evidence, the evidence now put forward by standard historians, and he would say, 'That's utterly ridiculous. That can't possibly be true.' Only because it has been accepted, it has a sense that it's true. But it really is preposterous. The idea that that man in the barn could have been Booth would not stand up in a court of law."

As convincing as Orlowek's evidence may be, Harmon's not budging.

"I hope the museum can hold its ground on this, and not allow the testing," said Harmon, "but if for some reason they can't, and the results come in, I hope the other side will finally accept the truth and move on. You know, everybody wants to make a conspiracy out of something. I don't know whether it's an American trait that we're born with, or what. But everybody's always looking for some sort of way to blame our government for something. But at a certain point, you just have to go with the facts."

Indeed, most of us in the civilized world are partial to facts. But as Prof. Kenzie explained, it's very difficult for even the most open of minds to escape confirmation bias: the tendency to ultimately believe the facts that confirm our personal worldview.

"Facts are the key to understanding history," said Kenzie. "I tell my students this all the time. Do I believe the government shot Booth in the barn? As of right now, I do. I tell them, I live right down the road from the barn. But historians need to be open-minded. The history of mankind is full of false conclusions, and if new information comes across your radar, and it's fact-based and sound, you need to consider it, even if it requires you to change your way of thinking. This type of mentality is what separates modern man from the cave man."

ONE-ON-ONE WITH ORLOWEK

(Online edition only – Sidebar)

BB: Can you give our readers one simple reason why they should doubt the "ending of record," if you will, of John Wilkes Booth?

NO: Well, for starters, the government's own expert, John P. Simonton, wasn't even sure that the man in the barn was Booth. In the nineteen-twenties, he wrote out a sworn affidavit saying that he had been in charge of all the documentation — which was kept secret for forty-five years. The evidence, in his opinion, did not show that it was John Wilkes Booth.

BB: But what about all the evidence and photos and people who identified the body as Booth that day at the barn?

NO: Several different people who saw that person at the barn and saw the body at later stages down the road, in terms of time, indicated that the person killed had reddish hair, had freckles. John Wilkes Booth had neither. He had jet-black hair, totally smooth complexion. Also, the body that was identified had various other marks on it that were not consistent with John Wilkes Booth. And all independent identifications of the man killed in the barn do not match up with the physical characteristics of John Wilkes Booth.

BB: How then do you square the evidence of the tattoo that was discovered on the corpse? Who else would've had the initials "J.W.B." burned into their arm? That sounds pretty convincing to me.

NO: The J.W.B. initials are frequently cited as proof the body was John Wilkes Booth,and our side does not dispute the real John Wilkes Booth had such a marking in life. It was common knowledge at the time. But with all due respect, of all the things in this epic case, that would be the easiest thing to correct. If they wanted that body to be Booth, they could have simply drawn the initials on. To me, the simple fact that everyone in the whole wide world knew about Booth's tattoo, actually qualifies it as the most dubious piece of evidence.

BB: I've heard some scholars say that in the years and decades following the assassination, many people came forward claiming that they were John Wilkes Booth. What can you say about that, particularly in reference to David E. George?

NO: There were other people who supposedly said they were John Wilkes Booth, and I've looked into all of those. None of those, however, I believe, are accurate. But they tend to take away from the authenticity of our evidence, because if you have twenty different people running around as John Wilkes Booth, nineteen of them — at least— cannot be John Wilkes Booth. The exhaustive work that all of us on my team have done indicate that he was not killed in the barn and that he ended up in Enid, Oklahoma territory dying in 1903.

Nate Orlowek is the chief researcher of the John Wilkes Booth escape research team. He has appeared numerous times on television, radio, and in print as a pre-eminent Booth expert, including NBC's "Unsolved Mysteries," History Channel's "De-Coded," CBS, ABC, PBS, the Philadelphia *Inquirer*, Rolling Stone Magazine, and NPR.

14

A STROKE OF FORTUNE

The week that followed the original post date of this story had to have been the most eventful of Daniel's life. The major news media gobbled it up, and his story launched a national debate on the subject.

All the pundits got in on the action, throwing their philosophical two cents in about the pros and cons of the exhumation like it was an election campaign. For multiple news cycles, the talking heads hypothesized up and down about the multiple potential impacts of the result on the population at large. One conservative cable-news host went so far as to say, "There might be a nuclear holocaust." But this was one of the more radical views out there. Most of the press covered the story with a healthy dose of skepticism.

Bill O'Reilly devoted a long segment to the topic on *The O'Reilly Factor.* Co-author of the recent book, "Killing Lincoln," the Fox News host took an unusually thoughtful tone when interviewing his guests on the subject, one of which was the renowned Booth scholar, Michael Kauffman, author of "American Brutus: John Wilkes

Booth and the Lincoln Conspiracies." I recognized him immediately by his perfectly cropped goatee.

I've known Michael for nearly twenty years, since 1995, when he famously testified as a Booth expert on behalf of the cemetery. To this day, I vividly recall sitting in the courtroom being thoroughly convinced by his testimony that Booth was shot in the barn. He made it seem so plain and simple. Michael is one of the most sensible guys you'll ever meet, and I thought Bill did a great service to the public by having him on his show. He added much needed perspective to the conversation, especially with regard to the legendary "Book of Bates."

As with most of the shows on television these days, I was able to dig up the interview from the show page archive and include a portion of it for you below.

O'REILLY: I've got a book here, Michael, which I know you are very familiar with. (producing the book) It's by Finis L. Bates and it's called The Escape and Suicide of John Wilkes Booth. Escape theorists point to this all the time as conclusive proof Booth got away. What's wrong with it?

KAUFFMAN: Aside from the fact it's probably the most amazing bald-faced flim-flam that I've ever heard of, not much. I mean, even the first sentence is so far off, historically, geographically. He just makes so many wild off-the-wall claims all the way through. I mean, this guy had a lot of nerve.

O'REILLY: Really? How so?

KAUFFMAN: Starting with the premise. In 1903 Bates, supposedly, heard about this man David E. George dying in Enid Oklahoma who claimed he was John Wilkes Booth. So Bates went out to Enid and said, "That's my old friend. He's the same guy I knew in Texas many years ago who confessed he was John Wilkes Booth." Then he and another woman, who claimed she was Booth's daughter, tried to claim the body and what they thought would be the great fortune he left behind.

O'REILLY: It turns out, he didn't leave a thing, right?

KAUFFMAN: Right, but they were fighting over it, until eventually Bates gave up and, somehow, acquired a dead body, which he said was David E. George, but really John Wilkes Booth, and he used this as proof that Booth had not been killed in 1865.

O'REILLY: But with all due respect, Bates did acquire a body, which is not easy to do, by the way, that happened to look an awful lot like John Wilkes Booth. How can you be so certain the corpse was not Booth?

KAUFFMAN: Because, if you actually go down into these places, like Texas and Oklahoma and Mississippi, like I have, you find out that David E. George who died in Enid, Oklahoma, was really David E. George. That was his real name. He had left his wife and three children back in Mississippi, and if you do just a little bit of digging, you'll find that when David E. George died, his brother-in-law contacted Finis Bates, who was David E. George's family attorney, and Bates went out to Oklahoma so that he could bring the body back to the family. But then he stuck all this business in there about John Wilkes Booth, and it all just blew up so fast that he ended up telling the family, "No, no, no. It's the wrong David E. George. It's not your guy." But it was the right David E. George. And Bates not only defrauded the public, but he defrauded the David E. George family who had sent him to Oklahoma.

O'REILLY: Do I understand this correctly? Bates published his account as non-fiction, complete with a bibliography and all. Yes or no?

KAUFFMAN: Yes.

O'REILLY: So then how come nobody investigated his research?

KAUFFMAN: You know, that's a good question. It sure beats me. I mean, this guy was violating laws left and right.

O'REILLY: Are you in favor of going ahead with the exhumation right now, to clear this whole thing up, once and for all?

PAUSE.

KAUFFMAN: You know, if the family wants to go ahead with it, who am I to stop it? If everyone can agree, in *advance, that the test to be performed would be conclusive, then I say fine. Go ahead with it.*

It was a startling, if reluctant, endorsement. Of course Michael was confident in his belief that Booth was killed in the barn, but he had sense enough to take the conversation seriously and conclude the only way to get closure on the subject would be to go ahead with the exhumation. Not all of his traditional-minded colleagues felt the same way.

The upside of the whole conversation for Daniel, of course, was that overnight he turned into a national celebrity. He became the go-to media expert everyone wanted to hear from. He appeared on all the talk shows. His name was in all of the newspapers. He even did the comedy rounds.

"Ladies and gentlemen, tonight's guest is a very unusual person," Stephen Colbert deadpanned in his introduction on *The Colbert Report*. "His name is Daniel Boland. You may have heard of him. He claims he is a distant relative of John Wilkes Booth. But that's not all. He says he comes here tonight with proof that John Wilkes Booth is also the great, great, grand uncle of Lee Harvey Oswald, who, it turns out, is the great, great, great, great, great, great, great, great, great, great, great, great, grand cousin of Napoleon."

As playful as Colbert's joke may have seemed, it was loaded with traps and pitfalls to snare Daniel. In this way, every interview he gave that week was the same. The miraculous thing was how deftly he walked the tightrope. In short, Daniel shocked the world.

He was mild in manner and appearance, personable and charming. Nothing about him seemed loony or crackpot. On the contrary, it was surprising to hear a conspiracy theorist sound so sane and lucid. He was eloquent, always speaking in calm, even sentences. He had it all perfectly worked out in his head. He spoke as if he were running for president, as if he was born for this single purpose, but that didn't stop journalists from trying to throw him off balance.

"At this point, isn't this all just a sideshow circus that distracts us from the more important legacy of President Lincoln?" was the gist of the most common criticism, quite justified I thought.

"Haven't we heard enough about Booth already?" was another popular one, to which Daniel would patiently reply something to the effect of, "Perhaps, yet the fact that the government has repeatedly put a stop to research for over a hundred years is highly suspicious."

Somehow, he managed to sound fresh and convincing each time. But in my opinion, Daniel's toughest test of the two dozen or so interviews he gave that week was the debate he had on *Real Time with Bill Maher* on Friday night.

Maher, who calls himself a comedian, not a journalist, is a more thorough reporter than most of the "legitimate" reporters you see on television. And because his show airs on HBO, he can cut through the usual bullshit often associated with prickly subjects like John Wilkes Booth, which is just what he did when interviewing Daniel.

Daniel was Maher's first guest of the evening. After his opening monologue, Maher enthusiastically introduced him, saying, "I've been looking forward to speaking with this guy all week." I'm sure he was. Maher is an outspoken critic of conspiracy theories. I watch his show regularly and I have never seen him once entertain one. To Maher, they're all the same, 9-11, Osama Bin Laden, global warming, and now Booth. I was nervous for Daniel. After welcoming him, and exchanging some comic banter about Booth, Maher got into it.

MAHER: I read your story, and you're a very persuasive writer, but I have to say, one paragraph, in particular, stuck out to me that I think just about says it all. It's a quote from a woman you interviewed from the Surratt Society. I have it right here. Her name is Jane Harmon. She's a professor of sociology. She says:

"Everybody wants to make a conspiracy out of something. True believers will always believe the world is flat and that John Wilkes Booth escaped."

To me, this hits the nail on the head. Why must we go through this every single time? To me, this is no different from the fanatic creationists. What do we have to do? What do we have to say to convince these people to accept basic, fundamental facts? Can you explain it to me? I'm really curious.

(Thunderous Applause.)

BOLAND: I'll tell you what I find more curious, how, of all institutions, the Surratt Society, the society Professor Harmon belongs to, came to be the center of conventional thinking on Booth's death. They don't admit to having an inkling of suspicion about any of it, even though the same Secretary of War, Edwin Stanton, who lynched their namesake Mary Surratt in one of the most corrupt military tribunals in U.S. history, that Edwin Stanton also churned out the report on Booth's death at the barn.

(Brief Pause.)

MAHER: Well, I don't know enough about that to make a comment. What I do know is that there is a ton of evidence to convince me they got the right guy. Look, the leg was broken in the same place as Booth. He had a scar on the back of his neck in the same spot as Booth did. He had a tattoo on his arm with the initials 'J.W.B.' I mean, come on. If it looks like Booth and smells like Booth, isn't it Booth?

(Laughter. Thunderous Applause.)

BOLAND: Those are all very good points, all good bits of evidence…

MAHER: I think they're a little more than bits, don't you?

BOLAND: Maybe so, but if you study both sides of the argument, I think you'll be hard pressed not to find reasonably compelling evidence in both directions.

MAHER: Come on.

(Laughter.)

BOLAND: I'm telling you, I've been researching this a long time.

MAHER: What do you think? Do you believe he got away?

BOLAND: I get asked this question all the time and after all my research, I really have to say, I have no idea.

MAHER: Come on!

(More Laughter.)

BOLAND: I'm serious. I honestly believe it's a fifty-fifty chance he got away.

MAHER: So you don't believe he got away?

BOLAND: I believe it's a fifty-fifty chance.

MAHER: Yeah, but if somebody put a gun to your head, no pun intended, and made you choose, what are you going to say? You're gonna say they got him, am I right?

(Hoots. Whistles.)

BOLAND: No, actually, if I couldn't say I didn't know one way or the other, I think I would have to say he got away.

MAHER: Really??

BOLAND: *Only because I believe, if you look at the entire case as a whole, with an open mind, there are too many red flags, too many inconsistencies.*

MAHER: *You would really take the bullet?*

(Laughter.)

BOLAND: *Yes, because, to me, it's as inconclusive as fossils and plankton.*

MAHER: *Huh??*

(Laughter.)

MAHER (CONT): *Did he just say plankton?*

(More Laughter.)

BOLAND: *I did. Bear with me a second. This is right up your alley.*

MAHER: *I'll be the judge of that.*

(Laughter.)

MAHER (CONT): *You better make it a quick second.*

BOLAND: *Isn't it ironic that Finis Bates, the guy who wrote the book on Booth's escape, wrote he first met Booth in, of all places, Glen Rose, Texas? Of all the places in this country, Glen Rose is home to both Dinosaur Valley State Park and the Creation Evidence Museum. The crossroads, if you will, of truth. One side of Glen Rose believes dinosaurs have been extinct for sixty-five million years, the other believes the earth is ten thousand years old. One side believes oil comes from dinosaur fossils, the other believes it comes from plankton.*

MAHER: So now you're bringing the Clampetts into this??

(Laughter.)

BOLAND: It would be entertaining to hear Jed Clampett's thoughts on Booth.

(More Laughter.)

BOLAND (CONT): No, but unlike plankton and fossils, unlike Lee Harvey Oswald, unlike Archduke Ferdinand, we can actually get to the truth. This may be our only window, perhaps in the whole history of mankind, to do an experiment of this magnitude, and they want to shut it down?

(Applause.)

MAHER: All right, all right already. I give up. You've convinced me. Go ahead with the damn thing, if it will shut the crazies up when the test shows they got the right guy. You'll come back and join our panel after it's all over, I hope?

BOLAND: It would be my pleasure.

MAHER: Excellent. Until then, Daniel Boland, everybody! Now it's time to introduce our panel.

(Applause.)

And just like that, it was over. The camera panned away and Daniel vanished. But his case had passed another critical test. It held up against tough scrutiny and continued its momentum into the weekend.

Of course, during all of this publicity, the Army Medical Museum was mostly silent. They were unreachable to the press, save a short token statement released from Elizabeth Colburn's office.

"A woman was killed recently in Bel Air, Maryland, at the old Booth homestead," Colburn's widely circulated statement read. "Our top intelligence officers have told us they have credible reason to believe going ahead with any testing at this time could seriously jeopardize national security. Therefore, presently, the museum has not changed its decision not to allow the testing." But by Sunday, the museum was forced to reconsider its stance.

In reaction to all the press, Congressman Christopher and Senator Frank came out on "Meet the Press" in favor of the testing, echoing Daniel's "This may be our only window" argument. Senator Frank said that there was bi-partisan support in both the House and Senate "to put this thing to bed, once and for all."

Then on Tuesday we all got the word.

It began that morning with a call from Elizabeth Colburn to Nate Orlowek. Nate then relayed the message to Daniel, who in turn relayed the message to me.

According to Daniel, the museum's board of directors voted overnight in favor of allowing the testing. Colburn would announce the decision, he said, that evening in an interview with Anderson

Cooper on CNN. Daniel was overjoyed. To celebrate he decided to throw a last-minute party at the Players, where we could all watch the interview on the big screen when it aired. Everyone he knew was going to be there, except, of course, anyone from the research team. They all lived too far away. But Penelope Jordan was going be there. And if Penelope Jordan saw fit to come, it had to be a worthy occasion.

"PJ," as she's sometimes called, is perhaps the most unsuspecting history professor in the world, given the fact that she's a young attractive vixen in a world largely dominated by old ugly men. She teaches at NYU and is a well-known provocateur. For this reason, reporters love her. She's often quoted in the papers and online as an expert in American history studies. Daniel interviewed her once for a Beacon story and for a brief period they dated, until she broke it off. After Daniel's Booth story ran, however, she took a renewed interest in him.

Before they joined everyone down in the pub that night, she orchestrated a photo shoot for Daniel in Gramercy Park, in front of Edwin's statue, to document the monumental decision. As I watched her snap away from the balcony of the club, I couldn't help but notice how at ease and confident Daniel seemed. Had he forgotten the tragic series of events that transpired just a week ago? If so, he wasn't the only one.

Ever since our debauched weekend, apart from Elizabeth Colburn's anemic reference to "the old Booth homestead" incident, poor Joan Stevens had become as obscure as Junius Booth. The police had yet to name a suspect in the murder. They still hadn't found her truck. And oddly there seemed to be nobody willing, or able, to come forward as a witness. I, myself, began to believe the whole thing never happened. Then again, maybe Daniel couldn't get Joan Stevens off his mind. We'll never know. All I can say is that as I observed Daniel that triumphant evening, he didn't even vaguely resemble the paralyzed Daniel who read the Sun in my convertible the day after her murder, panicked he would be picked up by the authorities any second. Soon, my curiosity subsided as well. I was sucked into the Booth vortex along with everybody else.

15

THE PARTY

It was a bumping party at The Players that night. It felt like the whole club had shown up to see the interview and wish Daniel luck. Everyone was there and in a good mood, eager to drink and laugh. Daniel held court at the same community table that Humphrey Bogart and James Cagney and Frank Sinatra and countless other greats occupied before him. With Penelope at his side, echoes of Debussy and Schumann seemed to serenade Daniel alone.

I sat at the end of the table next to Jake Gillam, a hilarious New York character actor, infamous in the off-off Broadway world. Jake is around my age and a congenial drunk. We hit it off the first time we met. Next to Jake sat the immortal Henry Taylor, ensconced in his hemorrhoid-cushioned throne.

"Lord" Taylor, as we like to call him, is an ancient English actor who has played the Ghost of Hamlet's father on Broadway more times than any other actor in history. He's also a former president of the club, a harmless-looking, doddering old man, who, I'm told, caused more harm to the club during his tenure than any other ten presidents combined. Watching him stoically sip his pint of Newcastle that night, I could tell the old ghost was oblivious to everything in his past. Fittingly, sitting next to him to remind him was Lord Taylor's young protégé, Lew Ploupfe.

A veteran Broadway flutist in his mid-sixties, Lew looks and talks more like an overweight butcher or a pirate than he does a delicate musician. After the board managed to boot Lord Taylor out of office, Lew was appointed the interim president for a while, until a suitable replacement was found. Luckily for all of us, that didn't take too long.

Lew is one of the few members of the club, including myself, who had followed the exhumation trial in Baltimore in the mid-nineties. Unlike me, however, Ploupfe has always been a Booth escape theorist and had been demoralized by the outcome of the trial for years. It shook the gelatin of his marrow.

When the court struck down the proposal, he was convinced there was a larger conspiracy behind the decision, an opinion he wouldn't hesitate to share with anyone who walked through the door. As soon as he would get a drink in him, he would unleash, without restraint, his rabid fears about our government, how they were going to take away all our guns, when God-knows-what might be out there.

During diatribes of this variety, he took on the traits of your textbook paranoid freak. I have always found it incredible how such a large and volatile man could play such a dainty instrument as the flute so well. I often wonder what his peers in the pit must think of him. I'm sure they could give me an ear load. On the night of

Daniel's party, he was in classic form, reveling in good cheer across the table from the guest of honor. He was beaming at the prospect of finally exposing the great lie. He couldn't suck down his gimlets fast enough. His face was as red as a thermometer, an observation Jake couldn't pass up.

"You better slow down there, Lew," Jake said. "It would be a terrible tragedy if you dropped dead of a heart attack now. And to keel over in Miss Penelope's spinach dip, that would just be plain rude."

To be sure, it was an amusing cast of characters there in the first rotation at the table. Of course all around us, and drowning out Lew's animated laughter, the pub was packed, wall to wall, with members drinking and laughing merrily. Every minute, it seemed, someone else stopped by the table to say hello to Daniel and ask him about the exhumation. Though I'm sure Daniel appreciated all the attention, it was quite clear, to me at least, he was terribly exhausted. All the running around had finally caught up with him and before long he couldn't help but show it. So for a change, everybody else did the talking, while he quietly sat in the corner, just below Al Hirschfeld's doodle of Edwin, and decompressed with his scotch.

In Daniel's place, Penelope kindly saw fit to sit in as the moderator. It was remarkable to witness. She slipped into the role of host of the evening as smoothly and easily as Katie Couric, asking pointed questions one moment and then earnestly summing up the communal consensus the next. All the while, Jake Gillam interjected absurd quips that caused Lord Taylor to grimace and scratch his head furiously.

"Just what are you saying, man?" our ex-president demanded at one point, to the hearty laughter of everyone at the table.

Then for a while there, the reigns seemed to slip away from Penelope. As I recall, the conversation took a strange turn, then transgressed before inevitably segueing into an old drinking story about Junius Booth and Sam Houston, which ultimately got Ploupfe rolling on the subject of the Houston conjecture.

"It was all arranged beforehand," he said with gusto. "Sam was John's godfather!"

I had debated Lew a hundred times over the years, but this time I just let him go. Why ruin his night, I thought. Besides, I knew before long, Penelope would bulldoze him. Sitting casually beneath Ray Kinster's portrait of the young and facile Katharine Hepburn smoking a cigarette and contemplatively staring off into the horizon, Penelope just as effortlessly tugged the conversation back in her direction.

"So tell me," she commanded, "what would have happened if Lincoln lived? If John hadn't succeeded? What would be different today?"

Of course, Lew tore into this impossible question first.

"Well," he said, choking back a belch, and I paraphrase minimally, "Everything! If Lincoln hadn't been killed, he would've brought the war to an end, properly. He would have been forced by the radical Republicans to stick it harder to the South."

"Seward would have likely been elected president next," Lord Taylor eloquently added.

"That's right," Ploupfe agreed, "And then Reconstruction would have properly been over sooner, and then Samuel Tilden would have most likely beat Rutherford B. Hayes in the election of 1876."

"God damn it, Gore would a' beat Bush!" Jake yelled and everybody roared.

We could all recite it perfectly. It was Lew's magnum opus. I wonder what it would sound like on his flute.

In any case, around the time Lord Taylor launched into a senile trip down memory lane, weaving in Lincoln history, here and there, like a blind driver knocking down construction cones on the highway, my bladder told me I had to take a leak.

"I still remember the day, as if it were yesterday, when my daughter Caroline came home and asked me seriously if Santa Claus was real," I thought I heard the president say on my way to the bathroom.

After I got out, I looked over at the table and saw him still talking, so I decided to jump ship. I thought it would be better to watch Penelope attentively listen to Lord Taylor's Christmas carol with a straight face from across the pool table. The large green light hanging over it was a good shield. It enabled me to play a round with David Copeland, the club sharpshooter. Every now and then Jake and I would make eye contact across the room and smile at the replacement cast at the table.

The receiving line for Daniel never ceased. All of the wise men paid homage, showering the babe with good tidings. Despite his questionable heritage, Daniel was the new heir apparent. He was the star who was going to make the Booths famous again.

Throughout the evening the noise in the pub swelled to near chainsaw-decibel level. Then at 7:59 pm, sharp, everyone in the pub abruptly quieted down and waited breathlessly for *Anderson 360* to begin. As David and I walked over from the pool table to the television, I bumped into Marilyn Betts. She seemed quite upset, but couldn't resist the urge to join in the party. I said hello and asked how she was doing.

"Fine," she answered dryly, "Thanks for asking," then turned away. Ever since that drunken night, she put me in the same box as Daniel. Daniel was a monster, or terrorist, out to destroy civilization as we know it and, therefore, so was I. But there was something more to it than that.

Observing Marilyn safely from across the room, she seemed to mirror the same stifled control Elizabeth Colburn displayed when she officially told Anderson Cooper, "Yes, the board made the decision to allow the testing late last night." It downright frightened me. For an instant I questioned whether or not Marilyn might actually be a spy, acting as the eyes and ears of the museum. Could it be possible, I wondered, before I chuckled and dismissed the possibility as preposterous.

"The museum is now of the opinion," Elizabeth continued, "we need to put this thing to rest, once and for all."

When Colburn's segment ended, jubilant applause erupted in the pub and everyone went over to Daniel and high-fived him and shook his hand, and then the real revelry began, and didn't stop until dawn. And true to Elizabeth's words, the museum did not interfere again.

THE LAST SUPPER

On Thursday, April 25th, all the major players, from near and far, made their way to Cambridge, Massachusetts, where the exhumation of Edwin Booth was scheduled to commence at Mount Auburn Cemetery at nine o'clock sharp the following morning.

The day after Colburn's announcement, the Smithsonian Institution had spoken up and graciously volunteered their resources to help manage "The Ultimate Scientific Expedition to Identify John Wilkes Booth," as it officially came to be known. Considering the Institute's impartial reputation, and the fact they agreed to foot the bill, both parties saw fit to let them arrange the operational logistics. From that day forward, the Smithsonian banner would be attached to any and all Booth theatrics.

First, Smithsonian officials arranged for Dr. Kay, the expedition's lead geneticist, to slice three tiny bone samples from the vertebrae of the man shot in the barn, which were kept at the National Museum of Health and Medicine, enough to manufacture ample control and backup samples. To ensure the greatest degree of accuracy, two identical laboratories had been selected to conduct simultaneous replica tests. In theory, they would produce the same conclusive results at the same time. After Dr. Kay completed her incisions at the NMHM, she took the primary sample with her back to the Institution's main lab in Washington, accompanied by a military escort. The primary control sample, meanwhile, was delivered via armed courier into the hands of the Smithsonian's chief geneticist, Dr. Fletcher Foley, at the Armed Forces DNA Identification Laboratory in Rockville, Maryland.

The Smithsonian hoped to accelerate the process, which ordinarily can take as long as six months when dealing with old skeletal remains like Booth's. On the eve of the exhumation, I heard one reporter on television say officials hoped to have a verdict as soon as a month later.

The representatives from the museum, I assumed, all flew in from Washington, but they could have taken a bus from Kansas for all I know. No one knew anything about the inner workings of that institution, which kept its procedures and movements strictly confidential.

As for the "Expedition," the radical team of researchers to which I was destined to belong, we were scattered all over the country. Daniel and I made up the New York contingent. Due to the heightened sensitivity of the occasion, only family and "essential" members of the expedition were invited to witness the disinterment. Given that I had known most of the team for over a decade and was responsible for bringing Daniel into the loop, I was included on the VIP list.

For added effect, Daniel drove up with his mother, who I had yet to meet at that point, the day before. By doing so, they managed to miss the horrible rainstorm that relentlessly pursued me all the way up the eastern seaboard.

The whole drive, I felt like I was speeding through a carwash. When I stopped in New Haven to gas up, the large portico overhead deflected four giant sheaths of water that surrounded me on all sides. Over the roar of the waterfall, I could still hear the sound of the Yale bells ringing in the distance. It felt like I was going to a funeral.

A few hours later I arrived in Harvard Square. I needed a drink to take the edge off. Daniel and his mother were staying at the same hotel as I was, so the plan was to hook up at the hotel bar for a pre-dinner cocktail once I arrived, then rendezvous with the rest of the team at a nearby restaurant for what would ultimately be our last supper, but the first part of the plan never materialized.

At 6:25 pm, about a half-hour before we were supposed to leave the bar for the restaurant, I got a text from Daniel telling me to meet him there. He had been delayed at the cemetery for some unknown reason. I didn't text him back, but I settled up my tab and walked over to the Casablanca on Brattle Street.

It didn't take me long to get there. I knew the restaurant well. My ex-wife grew up in Cambridge and we used to go there when we visited her parents, who still live in the area. It opened back in the fifties and, despite changing owners multiple times over the years, has maintained much of its romantic charm.

The restaurant's main attraction, aside from the attractive Harvard grad students, is the giant mural painting that stretches dramatically across the dining room. Painted by David Omar White in 1970, it's a striking tableau of all the main characters in the film "Casablanca" starring Players-emeritus, Humphrey Bogart.

By the time I got there, the rain had stopped, but it was still damp and cloudy. Standing outside the front door of the Casablanca, I was paralyzed for a second. What if I ran into someone I knew? My ex-laws, perhaps? Then it occurred to me that the ex-laws were likelier playing badminton in Esmeraldas this time of year than going out to dinner in Cambridge and, thankfully, my blood pressure dropped.

When I walked in, the first person I met was Peter. He was by the coatroom scratching his ass. The minute he saw me, he started shouting obscenities.

"Well, I'll be damned," he said. "You made it, you old damned sallow cunt," or something to that effect.

He asked me what I was drinking, and we segued to the bar. To our surprise, Nate was already there. I hadn't seen him in person for at least ten years, so our hellos were a little more drawn out than normal.

"As I live and breathe, it's Nate Orlowek," I said.

"Al Pearson," responded Nate with a big smile. "How are you?"

I chuckled and thought briefly about how I should answer.

"I won't lie," I said. "I've been through the ringer, but I'm hanging in there."

"Oh, you don't look all that bad."

"That's very kind of you. How about yourself? What have you been up to, besides all this?"

"Busy, busy teaching, but apart from that, you said it. It's been all Booth."

"I hear that. Speaking of which, is anyone else here yet from the team?"

"As far as I know," said Nate, "We're the only ones. But that doesn't mean there isn't someone else here that I failed to recognize."

Nate was always careful like this with his words. He was never glib, even off the record, as Daniel was occasionally prone to be. Every sentence was precisely measured to convey, as accurately as possible, his exact opinion on a given topic. He had been trained to do so by forty years of speaking about Booth.

Nate was the true mastermind behind the project, the prime mover who had been patiently pushing it along all these years. He began researching the Booth escape theory as a teenager back in the early seventies after he read a book called "The Web of Conspiracy" by Theodore Roscoe.

"I became fascinated by the way Roscoe described the possibility that Booth escaped as 'a puzzle for history,'" he told us over a couple rounds of beer. "For the first time it occurred to me that history, as it's written and accepted, might not necessarily be true."

Today, at fifty-five, bespectacled, his hair thin and deeply receded, he is the world's pre-eminent scholar on the John Wilkes Booth escape theory, and the reason we were all gathering that night. The genesis of the exhumation could be traced back to an "Unsolved Mysteries" episode he famously took part in back in the early nineteen-nineties.

According to Nate, a couple of years before the special aired, he happened to hook up with an old history professor from the University of the South named Dr. Arthur Ben Chitty who had been researching the plausibility of Booth's escape since the fifties. Shortly after meeting Nate and comparing notes, Chitty invited Nate to take a trip with him to Enid, Oklahoma, the Mecca of the David E. George mummy. Nate agreed, and that trip became the impetus behind the 1991 "Unsolved Mysteries" double feature on John Wilkes Booth. Nielsen estimated over thirty million viewers tuned in.

In the documentary, Nate and professor Chitty squared off against James Hall, author of the official, Surratt Society-sanctioned Booth Escape Tour that Daniel and I took earlier that spring. Moderated by Robert Stack, the two opposing camps sniped at each other, firing off rounds of facts and counter-facts, leaving the audience baffled about what to believe. The documentary ended with a haunting vision of the Booth family plot in Baltimore. The narration that accompanied the images suggested the only way to know the truth, for sure, was to use modern science to identify the remains of the man shot in the barn.

Standing next to Nate at the bar on the eve of Edwin's exhumation, Chitty and Hall long dead, I couldn't believe the day had finally come.

"Mazel tov!" I said and raised my glass. "You finally did it."

Nate smiled broadly.

"Mazel tov!" he replied. "I see you've been practicing your Hebrew," to which Peter and I both laughed.

When not howling at the Booth moon, Nate works as a renowned Hebrew teacher in, of all places, Silver Spring, Maryland, just up the road from the National Museum of Health and Medicine. In fact, he told me, the reason he didn't answer Daniel's call that afternoon we left the museum was because, at the time, he was in Tel Aviv giving a lecture. Soon, the conversation turned to the trial of '95.

"Think," Nate said, reflecting on the "Battle of Green Mount," "If we would have won that case, we might not be here today."

Looking back, I think Judge Kaplan made the right decision in denying the exhumation request. Before the advent of DNA testing, there was no reliable way to identify the body. If Kaplan had let them go through with it and it failed, they never would have gotten the chance to test the vertebrae.

As we recounted all this history and hypothesis, Daniel finally arrived on the scene.

"Daniel," I said when I caught sight of him. "You made it."

"I made it all right," he said. "You'll never believe what happened." He looked overjoyed. "They almost stole Edwin," he said with a beaming smile.

After a brief pause, Peter asked, "What the hell do you mean they almost stole him?"

"Exactly what I said," Daniel replied. "They almost robbed Edwin's grave!"

Apparently, the previous night, Edwin came within a smoot of becoming the most famous hack in MIT history. Just down the Charles River from Mount Auburn Cemetery in Cambridge, the students at the Massachusetts Institute of Technology have been perfecting pranks, popularly known as "hacks," since at least 1958, when fraternity brothers from Lambda Chi Alpha used freshman pledge Oliver Smoot's 5.58333-foot frame to measure the length of the Harvard Bridge, 364.4 "smoots," plus or minus one ear, in case you were wondering. My personal favorite was when a group of students stole a campus police car, took it apart, piece by piece, and then reassembled it on top of the great MIT dome, then dressed a crash dummy in a police uniform, put it in the driver's seat with a box of donuts on its lap, turned on the siren, and locked all the doors. It took two days to get the thing down.

I wonder what would have happened if the hacks that attempted to steal Edwin's skeleton that night had succeeded. They came close. The plan had been brilliantly orchestrated by a band of engineers from the MIT fraternity Phi Alpha Tau, or "PAT" for short. After they dug up the grave, the plan was to carry Edwin's coffin to the river and row it down the Charles, then off load it into a "Bean Town" trolley they had procured in the Back Bay, and drop it off on the front steps of Paul Revere's old house in the North End with the message "Special Delivery" taped to the top. While it certainly would have taken the prize for the most macabre hack in American history, you can't say it wasn't creative.

"The police sergeant I spoke to," Daniel told us, "said he believed they wanted to get caught."

Maybe so, but the cemetery wasn't going to take any more chances. Apparently an armed guard named "Bones" had been tasked to keep watch over the grave overnight. Daniel interviewed him that afternoon, which is what delayed him that night.

"Here's what he looks like," Daniel said, before showing us all a photo of Teddy Page on his iphone. Teddy was black and looked to be in his mid-fifties with heavy bags under his eyes. Because of the intense rain, he was also wearing a navy-blue poncho over his head to keep dry. Daniel happened to catch "Bones" in mid-sentence, or mid-chew, voicing what appeared to be sincere discontent of some sort.

I glanced up and saw the first of "the descendants," as Daniel frequently called them, walk into the restaurant.

"Are you guys gonna keep lookin' at porn," Kathy Beards, the outspoken great-great-great-grand cousin of John and Edwin, exclaimed from across the room, "or are we gonna get something to eat?"

"Great to see you too Kathy," said Pete. But Kathy refused to be subdued.

"Don't start with me, you shit-licking red-neck," she shouted. "I went through hell to get here, so I'll tell you right now, if this food sucks, I'm gonna take it out of your ass." Apparently Peter and Kathy had bickered for days about the choice of restaurant that night, before Peter eventually won out. This was Kathy's way of reminding him she would be turning in a review.

Kathy is a firm proponent of the shoot-first-ask-questions-later approach to interpersonal communication. How this short wiry woman amassed such a powerful arsenal is a mystery. The few times I've been in her company, I've found her ability to unnerve the most stoic of men uncanny. After Kathy loudly wrangled everyone in our party into submission, the hostess nervously pointed us to our table and then disappeared. Fortunately, I managed to evade Kathy's fire most of the evening. While she was off on her first mad rampage, I had the pleasure of meeting Daniel's mother, the lovely Margret Alice Wood.

Daniel hadn't spoken about her much. Peggy, as she prefers to be called, looks much younger than her years, a likely result, I found out at the bar, of her active lifestyle. She rides horses nearly every day and has been doing so since before she can remember. It's in her blood. Her father had owned and boarded horses on the family farm his entire life, as did his father before him. In fact, the family tradition dates back a couple generations before the Civil War and continues to this day. When Peggy's father and mother passed away, she inherited the farm and, subsequently, all its demands, which she insists she finds extremely rewarding.

I was surprised to discover how interested I was in her stories. She was a very engaging woman. I didn't want the conversation to end, but soon enough the meeting was called to order. The eight apostles of Booth, including myself, sat down at the table for the last time together.

The configuration was fairly straightforward. The table sat three people on each side and one at the head and foot. On this occasion, Lois Grossman sat at the head of the table. She was unmistakably the guest of honor.

At sixty-two years old, Lois can best be described as a pair of large glasses peaking through thick chestnut-colored bangs. I will always have a soft spot for Lois. I can't tell you how much she reminds me of my mother. I can tell you she is the long lost Anastasia, if you will, of the Booth family. Nate discovered her twenty-one years ago. She is the great-great granddaughter of Edwin Booth, descended from his sole surviving offspring Edwina and her husband Gnatius Grossman.

During the first exhumation attempt at Green Mount, one of the earliest obstacles the team had to overcome was getting approval from the Booth family. The cemetery demanded that all alleged descendants prove they were legitimately related by providing original birth and death certificates and certified genealogical charts, etc. To satisfy this request, Nate began a campaign to track down as many descendants as possible. He put ads in all the major newspapers, *The New York Times*, *The Washington Post*, *The Boston Globe*, *The Baltimore Sun*, and so on. Daniel's grandmother may have read one of the ads, which may have prompted her to tell him about his heritage. But there's no question, this is how Nate found Lois.

Until the day Lois met Nate she knew very little about her uncle John, let alone the escape theories. She had been raised in a house that revered Edwin. "Growing up," she said, "the name John Wilkes was never allowed to be spoken in the house."

Lois may have learned more about her great uncle sooner, but her mother died when she was a teenager, and when Lois's father remarried, the influence and memory of the Booth side of her family nearly disappeared. But when Lois caught sight of Nate's ad in *The Boston Globe*, she decided to reclaim her identity.

Lois is not a big talker. If Nate is overly specific with his speech in public, I would call Lois extremely cautious and reserved. If she doesn't feel she has something substantial to add to a conversation, she's content to remain silent. The night at the restaurant, Kathy, who sat to her left, did most of the talking.

"What I want to know is how this is all gonna shake out," she said. "What if they pull the coffin up and it falls apart?"

Nate interrupted her.

"I can assure you, Kathy, nothing like that is going to happen," he said. "Tell her Erin."

Everyone turned and looked to Dr. Erin Kay, who would ultimately saw off Edwin's bone and conduct the test. She sat between Peggy and Kathy at the table.

My impression, which most certainly was distorted by Peter, who sat to my left, was that she was a very quiet person by nature. When her soup arrived, she craned her head into the bowl and methodically spooned it up, all without making eye contact with anyone, as if no one else was at the table with her. But now she was pressed to answer Nate's question.

"Oh, no," she said, her face beet red, "The procedure is not invasive at all. The sample won't be larger than an inch-by-inch squared," and held up her thumb and index finger at eye level.

A long awkward pause followed until everyone recognized that no more details would follow.

Note, simplicity and brevity are invaluable commodities for the scientist. If only they were used more frequently in other disciplines.

All evening, the food and wine flowed freely. Wedged between Daniel and Peter towards the end of the table, I sat across from Peggy, Dr. Kay, and Kathy. In between sips of wine, I mused at how perfectly they blended into the Casablanca mural behind them. It seemed there was plenty to talk about, from baseball to damask curtains to the thwarted grave robbers. According to Daniel, their names were Hagar, Pogo, and Rothschild, but those were surely their fraternity aliases. And of course, sitting next to Peter, I got an ear-load of filthy Confederate jokes, which I won't attempt to repeat.

The supper officially came to an end when, at last, Kathy put her fork and knife down. "Damn, those were some good chops," she said, licking her lips. "I'm sorry I ever doubted you, P."

We all lingered at the table, as if we knew instinctively something more still needed to be said.

Finally, over coffee, Nate tapped his water glass with a spoon and stood up and spoke the only true ceremonial words of the evening. I assume Daniel copied them down. I never saw his "supper" notes, but he was scribbling continuously throughout the speech.

"I want to take a moment to thank everyone here for everything you've all done over the years," Nate said graciously. "I can't believe we're all here right now, on the eve of this. But I especially want to take this time to thank Lois, because without her approval of all this, none of this would be happening."

Everyone said, "Here, here!"

"We might very well re-write history in the following months," he continued and, as usual, I paraphrase a bit, "then again, we might not. Either way, the country will be better off as a result, and we will all be a part of history for seeing it through. This is what being a historian, or scientist, is all about. So thanks again for coming and being a part of this. I'm very much looking forward to tomorrow and hope you all are, as well."

"Here, here!" we all said again, and toasted. Before I knew it, the waiter brought the check and I signed my name and then, in a blur of coats and purses, everyone walked out.

I vividly remember stepping outside. It couldn't have been much after 9 pm, but the conditions had improved rather dramatically. The rain had stopped, and the clouds had cleared enough to reveal a bright full moon shining over Harvard Square. We all pointed it out, but Daniel spoke up and quickly corrected us.

"It's actually a waxing gibbous," he said, "but tomorrow night it will be full."Daniel went on to tell us that, in fact, the next day the second-shortest lunar eclipse of the century would take place and that it would last, roughly, four hours.

"The shortest won't happen until 2042," he elaborated. "That one will last only twelve minutes."

"Well, I'll be damned," Kathy said, and everybody stood there in the moonlight a few minutes more marveling at the wonder of the universe. It truly felt as though we had been divinely pre-selected to witness the universe reveal itself and then, oh, what we would know then.

Looking back on this moment, I can't help but wonder if perhaps we were.

17

THE BIG DIG

I left the hotel for the cemetery a little after eight the next morning. We were all supposed to meet at the Brattle Street entrance at 8:30 sharp, then head up to the grave together. Ordinarily the ride to Mount Auburn would have taken five minutes, but traffic was unexpectedly thick. Thankfully, without a minute to spare, the giant archway came into view and I saw Daniel waiting out front.

As I drifted that last stretch to the entrance, it was easy to blend in to all the chaos that surrounded him that morning. It looked like a crime scene. There was a police car out front with lights flashing. News trucks were parked on the curb and across the street. Geraldo Rivera was standing out front with a microphone in his hand. All around, pedestrians and cyclists and drivers, like myself, were gawking and talking and twittering about what was going on. Luckily, a traffic cop was there, waiving everyone along. When I pulled up to him, I told him I was on the exhumation team and pointed over at Daniel and he got his attention.

Daniel looked over with a dull gaze then smiled when he saw me. He nodded to the cop, who kindly let me turn into the entryway.

"It's absolute madness here," Daniel said, above the hum of the crowd when I pulled up next to him.

I asked him if I was the last one to get there. I was relieved when he answered no.

"We're still waiting for Lois," he said.

"She must've got caught up in the traffic too," I said.

Daniel chuckled and said, "Did you get a look at the chopper?" and pointed up.

I followed his finger and, sure enough, the local news helicopter was circling overhead.

"Un-fucking-believable," I said.

Poor Lois. All she requested was that everything be done as discreetly as possible and now there was a fucking helicopter flying over Edwin's grave. For an instant I thought of Marilyn Betts' heart breaking watching Geraldo back at the club.

According to Daniel, management couldn't keep the general public out of the cemetery itself, given its national landmark status, but apparently they were able to cordon off Edwin's section of the property and put roadblocks up along the inner-roads that led to the plot.

"They're only letting authorized people in," he said. "No press allowed. They're going to escort us via motorcade as soon as Lois gets here."

Daniel walked me over to the main gate and told the security guard I was authorized to pass. Somehow he had managed to establish a degree of credibility with the cemetery personnel.

As I drove through the granite portal, Daniel pointed me in the direction of the caravan, which extended beyond my field of vision and was reminiscent of a funeral procession.

"Pull up right there," he said, pointing to a big black Lincoln at the end of the line. "I think that's Chandler and Colburn. If it is, I want to watch them drive up."

I followed Daniel's instructions and parked behind the black town car, but couldn't make out Chandler or Colburn. The windows were completely shaded. They could have had a lion in that car and I wouldn't have known it. Luckily, there were plenty of other creatures to look out for as I waited for the procession to begin. For instance, the slowly increasing number of photographers who boldly crept and flocked and hung from trees and, literally, went out on a limb to try and snatch a piece of the action with their rapid-fire weapons.

Mount Auburn is truly the Harvard of cemeteries in the U.S. Founded in 1831, it is the predecessor to Oakwood and Laurel Hill and Green Mount and Green-Wood and all the rest of the wooded ivy-league cemeteries in the country that redefined the concept of a final resting place as a somber Garden of Eden. Experts claim the cemetery's landmark design inspired the work of Frederick Olmstead. Everywhere you turn flowers and trees and bushes and birds, and, that morning, reporters, stretched across acres and acres of rolling hills.

I confess, for a few minutes, I felt like I was in heaven. All that was missing was a harp. My bliss was shattered the moment Daniel knocked on my window and told me Lois had just arrived and that he was going to go up and tell the president of the cemetery that everyone was now accounted for. A couple minutes later, Daniel came jogging back, a little out of breath, and hopped into the passenger seat.

"Where's your mother?" I asked him after he shut the door. "Why aren't you driving up with her?"

"She's riding with Kathy," he said, "which is a relief. She can entertain her. I'm just too busy right now. I'm jumping out of my skin."

"Oh," I said. "When did all this start?"

Daniel had arrived before sunrise.

"Everything was quiet then," he said. "I brought Bones a cup of coffee and we watched the sun come up over Edwin's grave. Everything was peaceful."

Around seven, they started hearing reports come in over Bones' radio about news trucks showing up at the front gate and, soon enough, the president of the cemetery had been notified and an emergency meeting was called at headquarters, which resulted in the security clamp-down I witnessed when I arrived.

"You think this is something," Daniel said, as the parade to the grave commenced. "Wait 'til you see the tent they've set up."

At a glacial pace, the cars pulled up to the intersection of Spruce and Mound Avenues and let their passengers off at the base of Anemone Path, a narrow trail that leads up a small hill to Edwin's plot.

Finally, the big black Lincoln in front of us pulled up to the path and the driver's door opened, but, to my surprise, it wasn't Chandler or Colburn who got out. Instead, a tall, very strange looking man emerged. Though dressed meticulously in a black suit and tie, something about his appearance and behavior seemed mysteriously sub-human.

He was big and muscle-bound, with thick brown hair. His neck, in particular, was unusually large. It appeared as though he couldn't move it, it was so stiff. And the way he inhaled through his nostrils when he first stepped out of the car, the way his oversized jawbone seemed to unhinge, and the arch of his brow furrow, it was as if he were sniffing oxygen for the first time.

After taking in the air, he moved to the back door of the car, opened it, and stood like a soldier as Richard Chandler and Elizabeth Colburn fluttered out, like bats let out of a cage.

Elizabeth looked confused and uncomfortable. Unlike the day before, the sun was bright and piercing. The sky was a deep colonial blue without a trace of a cloud on the horizon, all of which seemed to offend Colburn's pale complexion. She wore dark sunglasses and seemed to shrink, as if she hadn't seen daylight in a very long time and might even be allergic to it.

Chandler looked much the same, but without the sunglasses. He squinted at the sun and dubiously looked around at the tombstones. I vividly recall Daniel's reaction.

"Did you see that?" he said, not so much to me, as to his ego, before quickly typing his observations into his phone. "I wonder if anyone else is here from the museum."

If there was, they didn't step out of that car. After Colburn and Chandler exited, the muscle-bound driver shut the door and swiftly returned to the driver's seat, then drove off into the cemetery instead of parking with the rest of the caravan.

I was the last person to pull up to the path. When Chandler and Colburn were about halfway up the hill, I told Daniel he should hurry out and follow them up. I parked behind the rest of the motorcade, in the spot that should have been Chandler and Colburn's, then hustled up the hill as fast as I could to catch up with Daniel. When I got to the top, however, he was nowhere to be seen.

At the top of Anemone Path, I discovered what Daniel meant when he said I had to see the "tent." In fact, it was a series of giant white canvass partitions that had been erected in a quasi-hexagonal pattern around the area of Edwin's plot. I couldn't help but chuckle. Although the tent provided a moderate degree of privacy, it was far from seamless. In some places there were large gaps between the fabric panels, especially where they met up with the giant orange backhoe that was planted at the far edge of the plot, leaving ample room for the more adventurous photographers to take their shots. And, of course, with the helicopter hovering above us, we were all exposed.

Nate's team squeezed tightly into one quarter around Edwin's headstone, while Chandler and Colburn and the Smithsonian representative stood in another, behind Mary's. The remaining turf was taken up by the president of the cemetery, his foreman, the back-hoe and its operator, along with "Bones" and the gravediggers, around Edwina and Gnatius's section.

Much to my relief, no sooner had I noticed the gravediggers' forest-green jumpsuits than Daniel popped out from behind a giant oak tree to direct me, yet again.

"This way," he whispered and led me around the tent and shrubs, past a black hearse guarded by two men in black suits who watched us very carefully as we passed to the bottom patch of the plot where, shielded from view by the back-hoe, I met Bones.

"You made it just in time, my man," he said. "Things are just about to get freaky."

That is how I became formally acquainted with Mr. Teddy Page, a former gravedigger, now the head groundskeeper of the cemetery. Instantly, I could see how he and Daniel hit it off.

Teddy was soon dishing out jokes, trying his damnedest to crack-up the gravediggers, who had to stand solemnly out front in the spotlight. One by one, he pointed them out to me and introduced me to them, intimately, from a distance. For the life of me, I can't remember any of their names, or their stories, but I clearly remember their eyes and stoic facial expressions as they silently leaned against their shovels and must have strained with all their might to subdue their inner laughter.

Daniel and I had the best view. From our station, we were able to observe all the backstage action, as well as the main characters, without drawing any unwanted attention to ourselves.

Save the sound of the helicopter, which thankfully muffled most of Bones' whispers, there was no overture to preface the big dig. There was no blessing. In fact, things were uncomfortably silent for several minutes before the foreman gave the word to the backhoe operator, Joe, to begin. With each clump of grass the steel claw grasped, we came that much closer to knowing the truth.

We were all holding our breath. None of us, including Bones, knew quite what to expect. What would Edwin's coffin look like? Was it made of pine or mahogany? Would it be large or small? Would it be intact or crumbling? How strong were the forces of decomposition, really?

Lois was anxiously rubbing her thumb back and forth over her wrist. Kathy looked like she was going to have a stroke. Even Elizabeth Colburn seemed on edge. Shaded by the giant oak tree coming into bloom above them, they all scrutinized every motion Joe made with his claw.

"Alas, poor Yorick!" Little did Edwin know what his destiny was to be in the afterlife.

Joe's work came to an end less than ten minutes after he began.

"All right, that's good, Joe," the foreman said with about three feet to go, then gave the signal to the gravediggers to get digging.

The three men stepped into the grave. Their shoveling was a thing to behold. The thought of digging a grave sounds terribly backbreaking, and judging from Bones, who had the posture of the letter "r," it is. But you never would have known it watching the trio who athletically dug the path to Edwin's bones that morning. In a screw-like pattern, they spiraled down to the coffin carving a series of fast disappearing steps into the earth that sounded like the steady beat of a maraca. They rotated down, flinging the dirt overhead in front of them. "So you don't hit the guy in back of you," Bones informed us, then let out a cross-eyed chuckle.

As they came closer to the anticipated depth of the coffin, their digging became more cautious. From where the gravediggers stood, it was very difficult to get the soil out, especially because it was so moist and heavy from all the rain the day before. The smell was quite musty, though Bones assured me it was much better than March soil, which is apparently the worst month for digging a grave.

With each tablespoon of soil they delicately pitched out of the grave, everyone seemed to inch forward a little closer to get a look. At one point I noticed the president whispering to the foreman who, in turn, appeared to relay the message to one of the gravediggers, who stopped digging and looked up at the khaki-clad foreman with an un-amused look on his face.

Apparently the foreman was reprimanding the digger for spilling too much soil on the virgin Mary's grave. I was too distracted to pick up on it at the time. By chance I happened to glance over at Dick Chandler and caught him involuntarily flinch at what must have been a bee or mosquito or some other pest trying to fly up his nose. I chuckled under my breath when he smacked his forehead, then closely examined his hand and the surrounding airspace.

The "Virgin Mary" Devlin was the love of Edwin's life. She was a beautiful young actress, who gave up a promising career of her own to begin a family with Edwin. Tragically, she died at the age of twenty-three, just two years after they married, leaving Edwin alone to raise Edwina, Lois's grandmother.

Edwin never recovered from the grief of Mary's death, in large part because he was to blame for it. Today the STD gonorrhea is well known and can be treated effectively with antibiotics. But back then it was a mystery. Men would often pickup the disease and show no symptoms at all and, therefore, be unaware they had it. As a result, many women in the nineteenth-century became infected. As with so many other injustices, women bore the brunt of that disease. Their systems reacted poorly to gonorrhea and, consequently, many of them died a long exhausting death. Mary Booth was just one of countless victims.

Edwin was crushed by her illness. I've been told that he was faithful to her until the end, that he had unknowingly become infected by the disease years before he met her. These facts, however, failed to console him. He couldn't bring himself to visit her on her deathbed. Instead, he drowned his pain in alcohol and tried to obliterate the whole wicked episode from his life. I can sympathize with him. Needless to say, it didn't work. He remained a deeply sad person the rest of his life. It's probably why he was so adept at playing Hamlet.

After an extremely painful mourning period, Edwin resolved to be buried at Mary's side for all eternity. She is the reason he was buried in Cambridge, instead of Baltimore with the rest of his family. And on the morning of his exhumation, his dirt was, yet again, soiling her garden. It was very touching, the president's sensitivity to Mary's memory, however inconvenient it was for the gravediggers.

Looking at her tall virgin-white headstone with a large cross carved into the center of it, I am certain Edwin wouldn't have wanted one blade of grass to be disturbed above her precious head.

Not long after the foreman issued his warning, at last, a light clunk echoed out of the grave. In response, everyone reflexively lurched forward to get a peek, but the foreman commanded them to step back.

"Let's let the diggers do their work. You'll all get a chance to look in a minute, but right now I don't want anyone to fall in the hole."

He actually said the word "hole." I don't know why, but for some reason it sounded so vulgar.

Somehow, these last moments of the dig went by both excruciatingly slowly and very quickly. As I waited impatiently like everyone else, I found myself focusing in on Edwin's tombstone. It's fairly modest in size, considering his social status at the time of his death, but on the front, there is a prominent, circular engraving of his profile gazing east, toward the rising sun. It almost looks like a giant green oxidized penny. Edwin Booth, 1¢.

Below, an epitaph reads, "Edwin Booth, Born November 13th 1833, Died June 7th 1893, I will turn their mourning into joy and will comfort them and make them rejoice from their sorrow. – Jer. XXXI 13"

Over and over again I repeated these words and numbers in my head, but the more I repeated them, the less sense I could make of them. As they circled my brain, the syllables detached from their meanings, and the whole bizarre scene in front of me began to spin in my mind's eye, Nate, Lois, Chandler, Colburn, Peggy, Kathy, Edwin's engraving.

In a blur, the gravediggers chiseled out the coffin. I have no memory of any sound during this period. Not the shovels, not the helicopter, not Bones, nothing, until, that is, one of the diggers brushed off the upper surface of the coffin with a broom, once it had been sufficiently freed from the soil that had smothered it for over a hundred years.

In that brush stroke all sound abruptly returned to the scene with a loud collective gasp, inhaled by everyone around the grave, as we all ignored the foreman's admonishment, including the foreman himself, and inched our way up to the edge of the hole.

Nate pressed his hand over his mouth. Peggy appeared to faint. If it wasn't for Kathy, she may have fallen face first into the grave. I can only imagine how the cameraman in the helicopter reacted.

"Holy shit," Bones said involuntarily.

Edwin's coffin was small and made of wood of a kind I couldn't identify, perhaps because it had been buried for so long. It appeared to be intact and sturdy. The coffin tapered from the shoulder-line to the feet, like an Egyptian mummy, which was a common style during Edwin's day. What was not common, however, was the tiny six-inch by six-inch window pane installed into the lid of the coffin above his face.

Through the dusty glass square, and the lens of FOX News, the world got a shocking close-up of Edwin Booth's hollowed-out skull.

He was unrecognizable, with no resemblance to the detailed engraving of his profile on his tombstone.

Thankfully, within seconds, the president of the cemetery had the sense to override the foreman and command the gravediggers to lift the coffin out of the grave as quickly as possible and load it into the hearse. Raw instinct seemed to grip the diggers as they hastened to follow the president's instructions, lifting the coffin to ground level, then deftly steering it behind the back-hoe and through the tent partition to the back of the hearse.

The gravediggers serpentined like soldiers on the field of battle, performing the swiftest medevac I'd ever seen, but in this case, the patient was already dead and the enemy fire came from a news chopper. As fast as the gravediggers executed their commands, the operation moved slowly enough to give each of us ample time to look deep into what used to be Edwin's eyes.

Of course, everyone present raced to follow them to the hearse. Peter and I were the last to arrive. Peter seemed uncharacteristically subdued, though at one point we shared a glance that seemed to say, what the fuck did we just witness?

This is how Edwin Booth resurrected himself from the earth, after a one-hundred-and-twenty-year rest.

After his coffin was securely loaded and fastened, Nate, Dick Chandler, and the Smithsonian representative gathered loosely next to the hearse and exchanged a few words. Daniel stood nearby to record them. Soon the group disbanded and Daniel walked over to

Peggy and whispered something in her ear, then spoke to Lois and Kathy, before walking over to me.

"Let's go," he said. "The hearse is going to wait for us down at the exit. From there, we follow everyone to the examiner's office." The hearse had already begun to gently roll down the rugged cemetery service road.

While the rest of the flock began their exodus down the hill to the motorcade, Daniel and I remained at the plot. Daniel had to wrap everything up. He needed to snap a few more photos and document the carnage left behind, the expressions of the president and foreman, who were now much more relaxed, and the gravediggers, who were scratching their heads, and of course Bones, who was chatting it up with Joe over Edwin's abandoned grave.

While I waited, I roamed around the back side of Edwin's tombstone and had a look. It bears a passage by Shakespeare:

"The idea of thy life shall sweetly creep into my study of imagination and every lovely organ of thy life shall come appareled in more precious habit more moving delicate and full of life into the eye and prospect of my soul, than when thou liv'st indeed."

18

THE COFFIN

After we all hooked up at the majestic gateway at the bottom of the hill, it took a concentrated effort for the motorcade to make headway through the tentacled mob that seemed to have doubled in size since I arrived just an hour earlier. Picketers were holding up signs with the stupidest slogans you've ever seen, things like "No Digging These Bones" and "The Bone Stops Here." Other protesters violently banged on our windows as we passed. To this day, I have no idea what riled them up so much. You would have thought we were representatives of some despot regime at a U.N. meeting, the way they behaved.

Whatever their gripes may have been, once we finally broke free of them, we took the most roundabout route you can imagine to get to our next destination. Left and right, and left and right again, we snaked our way seemingly through all of Cambridge. It was like we were trying to ditch a tail, which in retrospect we probably were. Several streets I knew pretty well from cruising the town all those years with El, but some passages baffled even me, and by the time

I could make north or south of them, our caravan abruptly began pulling into a parking lot I had never seen before.

Traveling in the last car in our motorcade to pass over the threshold, my nerves were suddenly shattered by the gnashing sound of the rickety gate that abruptly jolted and began closing behind me. It was a rusty old thing with more than a few pins loose and several wheels in desperate need of oil. It howled offensively for a solid three minutes before it finally latched shut, by which point I was parked at the end of a long row next to the others at the rear of a monstrous industrial building. I clearly recall a line of angry-looking loading docks on one wing of the building and about a hundred drooling air conditioners protruding from the other. Was it a government building, or did it belong to some other independent institution, like Harvard University perhaps? No one knew and I never did find out.

By the time Daniel and I got out of the car, everyone was walking toward a tiny staircase opposite the loading docks at the other wing of the building. It led up two flights to a single steel door. As a matter of precedent, I was the last to file in. Before I entered, I turned and looked around to take in the surrounding scene. There wasn't a living being in sight, which was consistent with the dominant theme of that day.

Following the group down another disorienting maze of inner hallways, Daniel and I eventually found our way to the previously-undisclosed "medical examiner's office." There, in "waiting room 3," through a large bulletproof window, we could all view Edwin's coffin laid out on a long stainless-steel table inside a white and brightly lit laboratory chamber.

When we arrived, Dr. Kay and her associate, Dr. Foley, were the only living people in the lab. For what felt like an hour, but in reality was probably more like fifteen minutes, they briskly shuttled back and forth between each other and their various instruments and electronic devices, fiddling with them endlessly, almost to the point of absurdity. Everyone in the waiting room, meanwhile, scrutinized their every motion with the utmost interest, not knowing when or how the main event would start. Nobody wanted to miss it. I couldn't blame them. We were all transfixed. No one knew how exactly it was going to go down. Personally, I thought everyone handled the situation well.

For years, the prospect had been so abstract, an extreme test of patience, of perseverance, of long-term thinking. Naturally, in the final stages of the project, as the last lines were being drawn in, we were all taxed. But now, Edwin was right there in front of us, staring at the ceiling through his tiny window.

Finally, the cemetery foreman appeared with a crowbar alongside the Smithsonian rep, who was there to supervise the operation, and he began to pry Edwin's coffin open. From this moment on, things transpired very quickly. It was an incredible thing to observe.

Had the foreman not acted so quickly and decisively in opening the coffin, it might have been the breaking point for the audience crammed in the viewing room. Lucky for us, we were spared any more drama. The foreman's hands were steady. With just a few swift motions he removed the lid and, when he stepped out of the way, the naked remains of Edwin Booth were, at last, revealed for all to see.

We all pressed our eyeballs against the window and stood on our tiptoes to get a good long look.

I cannot lie. The vision was shocking, Edwin's skeleton lying there like that. But contrary to what you might see in a horror film, there were no maggots or worms or other insects wiggling around in his ears. Any maggots there might have been crawling around his coffin at one time or other had long since departed. No, by the time the foreman came around to opening it up, there was very little left for any organism to feast on. At that point, the great Hamlet was little more than broken bones, barely held together by a leathery mass of black flesh. Very little clothing was left, apart from the soles of his shoes. They were surprisingly well intact. The interior lining of the coffin had all but vanished completely.

Assimilated in a thick layer of soil as he was, it was nearly impossible to imagine that the skeleton lying there in front of us on that stainless-steel table ever had the strength to save the life of Abraham Lincoln's eldest son Robert Todd in New Jersey, just months before John Wilkes killed his father, but it did. It's truly a strange, but true story. Robert retold it many times to many people during his lifetime and marked it down for all posterity in a famous letter he sent to a friend years later.

"The incident occurred while a group of passengers were late at night purchasing their sleeping car places from the conductor who stood on the station platform at the entrance of the car," Robert Lincoln wrote. "The platform was about the height of the car floor, and there was of course a narrow space between the platform and the car body. There was some crowding, and I happened to be pressed by it against the car body while waiting my turn. In this situation the train began to move, and by the motion I was twisted off my feet, and had dropped somewhat, with feet downward, into the open space, and was personally helpless, when my coat collar was vigorously seized and I was quickly pulled up and out to a secure footing on the platform. Upon turning to thank my rescuer I saw it was Edwin Booth, whose face was of course well known to me, and I expressed my gratitude to him, and in doing so, called him by name."

The unlikely event certainly makes one wonder about fate and destiny in this all-too-random-seeming universe. While I mused about whether or not there might actually be some higher intelligent design out there that we can't even begin to comprehend, Dr. Kay moved in on Edwin and cut into his right femur bone with her dremel and lifted up the first fragment for us all to see. Peggy visibly winced at the sight.

The best place to extract a DNA sample from a skeleton is from one of the weight-bearing bones, such as the legs and feet. The larger the bone, the more cells you have to work with. Dr. Kay told me on a previous occasion, her favorite place to extract from is the femur bone, which is just what she did again, a few minutes later, when she cut another sample from Edwin's skeleton and passed it over to Dr. Foley, who carefully stowed it in a military-grade container.

Shortly after her last incision, Dr. Kay took off her gloves and washed her tool and her hands and went back to her computer for several more minutes, while Dr. Foley and the cemetery foreman engaged in what appeared to be a lengthy casual conversation about

God only knows what. Meanwhile, the conversation inside "waiting room 3" was virtually non-existent.

Inside our chamber, everyone was wide-eyed, but nobody seemed to have anything to say. This may have been, in part, due to the various conflicts of interest swirling invisibly around the room like dark matter, but mostly I think everyone was in utter disbelief at what had just transpired. For Christ sake, they just dissected Edwin.

Lois and Nate looked as pale as Elizabeth Colburn. Peggy looked green. Kathy tried to stir up some conversation with her, but surprisingly Peggy seemed incapable of engaging. In fact, it appeared as though she was doing all she could just to prevent herself from throwing up on the spot. As for her son, he was too busy jotting down notes and taking photos, as usual, to talk or notice anyone at all, which was a funny irony, I thought, for a reporter.

With respect to the outliers in the room, those of us silently observing it all from a distance, in the shadows, Richard Chandler was definitely the most conspicuous. He lurked off in a corner and consulted his blackberry frequently, looking up at the rest of us seldomly, the President within arm's reach the whole time. Peter and I, meanwhile, camped out on the sidelines across the room, as far from the reach of Chandler as possible.

The whole scene was incredibly awkward. Thankfully, it didn't drag on that painfully long. Dr. Kay emerged fairly quickly from her laboratory after the dissection was completed. With a clipboard in hand, she told everyone that the samples of Edwin had been successfully taken and now she and Dr. Foley were ready to draw blood from the descendants, at which point everyone turned and looked around.

Seconds after Daniel's blood was drawn, the Smithsonian rep. grandly swept into the center of the room and thanked us all for coming. His face was remarkably tan and shiny. He told us that all the objectives for the day had been successfully met, and that Dr. Kay and Dr. Foley would be leaving the facility immediately to begin the extraction process at their dual labs in Washington and Rockville and that we should all begin exiting the building as soon as possible.

"We expect to have the results within a month's time," he said. "But as we get closer to meeting our objective you will all be among the first to be notified. I imagine you'll all need ample time to make travel arrangements to be there for the announcement in Washington."

Ample time, indeed.

"Now before we adjourn," he thoughtfully continued, "do any of you have any other questions you would like to ask me at this time?"

After a reasonable silence, the rep. took it to mean there were no more questions and so promptly dismissed us from the room. By that point, we all knew everything we needed to know. Edwin would remain in the laboratory until the following morning, when his remains would be re-interred at the cemetery, in a new coffin. After that, there was nothing more to do but wait, again.

In the parking lot, we all said our goodbyes. It was a happy farewell. Everyone was upbeat. The general consensus was that we all really accomplished something important that day. "See you in Washington soon," they all said, then got in their cars and went their separate ways.

I drove Peggy and Daniel back to the hotel. When we got there, Peggy said she wasn't feeling too hot and just wanted to crash in the room and watch a movie and order room service. "I can't remember the last time I did something like that," she told us. And so the moment the elevator doors closed on her, Daniel and I commenced our trip without any guilt to the nearest open pub.

With the world standing by as it was and forced to hold our breath as we did, what else was there to do?

19

THE PARTHENON

It was dark inside. The only light came from the sunrays that beamed in through the front windows. They stretched maybe a quarter-way across the barroom floor. The rest of the place was darkly cast in shadows. Daniel loved it. He called over to the bartender, who was too busy icing down the bar to notice us at first, and asked him if we could sit down and get a couple beers.

"Sit wherever you like," he said.

Apart from the bartender, we were the only ones in the place. We settled on a small table at the edge of the sunlight and before I knew it we both had a pint of Sam Adams in our hand. Gradually, we soothed our nerves with it to the tune of John Coltrane's sax, which had been serenading us from the moment we walked in the place.

The music really hit the spot. I never saw Daniel so absorbed before. He didn't say a word to me for quite a while. He just slowly bopped his head and tapped his foot in silence to the beat, breaking only to take a sip of his beer. It was impossible to know what he was thinking. One moment he looked contemplative. The next, he had a big grin. If I had to guess, I would have said he was clearing his mind, maybe even meditating after everything that happened over the course of the month. It was the first time all day I hadn't seen him with a phone or pen and pad in his hand. Sitting at our little circular table, tapping his foot to the rhythm, Daniel was a composer, not a writer. It wasn't until the music slowed and softened and we ordered another round that he began to return to Cambridge, and when he did, he acted as though I had been following right along with him in his mind the whole time, like an extension of his consciousness.

"What do you say we go to PAT?" he announced out of the blue note, as if I knew what the hell he was talking about. "The fraternity of those kids who tried to rob Edwin's grave," he explained. These were the first real words he'd spoke to me since we left Peggy off at the elevator.

"What for?" I asked him.

"I don't know," he said. "I'm kind of curious to find out what happened to them. I mean, they could be in jail right now, for all I know. I should at least follow up. It can't hurt."

I truly believe this is how he originally conceived the idea, vague and benign, another jocular adventure, a harmless distraction to take his mind off the looming results.

"We're not far from MIT, right?" he said. "I bet their house is nearby." Boy, did he calculate that one wrong. I should have taken the bet. If only he had any money. It turned out that the PAT house wasn't in Cambridge at all. It was across the river in Boston in the

Back Bay. "You up for a walk?" he said when he discovered this. "We can stop off for a pint anytime we get thirsty or have to take a piss?"

"You mean like a pub crawl?"

"You have anything better planned this afternoon?"

With the beer coursing through my veins as it was, and often does, I felt a false sense of invincibility. And I suppose I was a bit curious to see these clowns up close.

"Why the hell not?" I said.

"That's the spirit. The exercise will do us good."

"But listen," I warned him, "If I drop dead of a heart attack, you have my permission to re-measure the Harvard Bridge with my corpse," to which we both laughed and toasted at the prospect, and off we galloped, or rather staggered, Boston bound, stopping off whenever the need arose, as promised, to drink and piss.

The journey was a keg of laughs. I hadn't laughed so hard in years. Tears were rolling down my cheeks a good portion of the trip, and Daniel wasn't any better composed. In vivid detail, we relived every minute of the morning, play-by-play. We just couldn't stop cracking up. It was all too much, Chandler and Colburn and their mysterious driver, and Bones and the foreman and the Smithsonian rep., who was forever clasping his hands together like a preacher, and, of course, who could ever forget the first sight of Edwin's surprise coffin window and the look of horror it inflicted on the faces of all those present?

"What on earth were they thinking?" Daniel said, with tears streaming down his face, before proceeding to describe some of the most hilarious details I've ever heard in my life.

At one point I was so choked-up I couldn't produce any sound whatsoever. I was painfully suspended between what felt like a colossal yawn and the hardest guffaw a human being could possibly produce. But as cathartic as all this laughter was, it was exhausting, and all the alcohol we consumed didn't pep us up any.

By the time we reached the Harvard Bridge, my feet were dragging. Midway over the bridge, I had to stop and catch my breath. I looked for a pub, but there were none to be found. Daniel laughed at the thought of a bar on a bridge in Puritanical New England, and then pulled out his phone, as if he were going to Google the address. Instead he alerted me to the time.

"Jesus," he said. "It's three o'clock. The lunar eclipse is probably at full peak by now."

I had completely forgotten about it. The eclipse wasn't visible in North America in the daylight, but that didn't matter to Daniel. He took a few moments to observe it anyway and jot a few notes down about it in his notepad. I was relieved. I needed the rest. Besides, it was a gorgeous day, the prettiest I'd seen all year. The trees along the Esplanade were finally in bloom, after the arctic winter, and there must have been at least a hundred boats in the Charles, rowing and sailing and otherwise cruising to and fro.

Probably around the time stargazers in Casablanca began to catch sight of the eclipse in Morocco, Daniel pointed out the words

"Half-way to Hell" painted boldly on the sidewalk, commemorating the midway point of Oliver Smoot's legendary voyage. We both laughed at the reference and viewed it as a sign it was time to press on, which is just what we did.

By roughly a quarter to five, after a few more pit stops, we found ourselves standing on the doorsteps of 353 Beacon Street, the home of Phi Alpha Tau since 1904. Daniel knocked on the front door of "The Parthenon" and within seconds a pale young man with a shaved head answered.

"Hi," Daniel said and introduced himself. I had no idea what he was going to say. "I'm a writer from New York in town documenting the exhumation of Edwin Booth for a book I'm writing. This is my associate, Dr. Pearson. You mind if we come in?"

Being completely caught off guard by Daniel's request, the young man who introduced himself as "Knave" reluctantly let us in.

"I understand a couple of your mates got wrapped up in some shenanigans the other day," he said.

It was the words "mates" and "shenanigans," I think, that convincingly disarmed the young freshman.

"I suppose you could say that," he answered with discerning eyes.

"By any chance, are they here now?" Daniel asked in a timid voice that prompted Knave to pause before answering, "Yeah, I think they're here."

"Well, is there any way then that you could tell them I'm here and I'd really like to speak with them? Tell them if they're reluctant to talk to me, I completely understand, but they have my word, I won't print a word of our conversation without getting their approval first. We can speak off the record the whole time, if they'd like. I'd just really like to talk to them."

It appeared as though Daniel's words were overwhelming poor Knave, but somehow or other he must have been processing them, because after he agreed to pass along the message and went up a long staircase in the center of the house, he returned about five minutes later and told us to follow him back up the same staircase. Daniel and I both looked at each other a bit surprised, I think, that things were progressing so smoothly, and then up we went to the upper floors of the brick frat house, following Knave's footsteps the whole way.

If I remember correctly, at what felt like three stories up he led us down a dark and narrow hallway. I say "felt like three," because in that building of irreverent engineers, one never knew for sure, but let's just say for the sake of argument it was down a dark hall on the third floor we followed Knave until finally we reached a dark wooden door at the end of it.

It was an odd looking door. The handle was quite a bit lower than ordinary, which may have been because the actual door itself was shorter than usual. It couldn't have been five feet tall, but what- ever height it was, Knave knocked on it gently with his knuckle a few times and a couple male voices yelled in unison, "Come in," and then he opened the door for us. The instant it swung open, we were greeted by a giant cloud of pot smoke. It was as foggy as Golden Gate Park in there.

"Hello," Daniel said to a young man with shaggy blonde hair and small round glasses, "Hagar," as we would later find out. He was sitting comfortably facing us in a swivel chair across the room. "You mind if we come in?"

"Not at all," he said, "but watch your step."

We both looked down and discovered that to get into the room, you actually had to climb down a short series of rungs that formed a ladder, like in a submarine.

"Thanks for the warning," Daniel said, and we carefully began to climb down the ladder into the oddest room I've ever seen in my life.

In one corner, a plush-velvet orange sofa appeared to hover in midair like an Edwardian spaceship. In another, a metal file cabinet hung upside down from the ceiling. And with each step we took down the ladder, the sound of wind chimes rang out transcendentally from God only knows where.

Once we landed at floor level, Daniel politely began to introduce himself, but before he could do so, Hagar quickly cut him off. "We know who you are," he said.

"You do?" said Daniel, surprised. The frat boy managed to throw him off balance first. It was a remarkable thing to witness.

"Yes," Hagar said. "We read your story online and have seen you on television."

"Oh. You have." Daniel was at a loss for any more words.

"There's no need to be ashamed," Hagar's Asian accomplice, also known as "Pogo," interjected. "We think he got away too."

Before our conversation continued any further, Hagar gestured across the room. "You can go now Knave," he said. "We're alright." After he left and closed the door behind him, Hagar told us, "He's the smartest kid in the whole damn house."

"You should see the work he's doing with sub-atomic particles," Pogo added. "And he's only a freshman."

"You don't say," Daniel said, awkwardly.

Suddenly it was just the four of us in the room and the chemistry felt strained. Pogo and Hagar glanced across the room at each other, as if they were both wondering who was going to start talking first. Finally, Daniel asked them if we could sit down, which proved to be a wise request. Had we not been seated for the unexpected twist in conversation that followed, who knows what would have happened? As over the course of the next hour, these two unshaven undergrads, casually dressed in shorts and t-shirts, completely blew our minds.

Before I begin my recap I should mention, as a disclaimer, that both Hagar and Pogo told Daniel ahead of time that they were comfortable with everything they said being on the record and, if need be, they could verify everything. With that out of the way, they quickly moved on to explaining why their third partner in crime "Rothschild" was not in the room with us.

According to Hagar and Pogo, on the ill-fated night at the cemetery, they had just made it to Edwin's grave when they suddenly heard the sound of sirens and saw the police lights flashing. They said they tried to run, but it was no use. The police came prepared with a canine unit that hunted them all down in a matter of seconds.

"It all happened so fast," Pogo said.

Once they were all cuffed, they were apparently all transported separately back to the police station for questioning. For Hagar and Pogo, at least, the interrogation was fairly civil.

"I just told them everything I knew," Hagar said. "I didn't try to be a hero or anything."

As for Rothchild's session, neither of them had a clue. After spending the night in jail, the authorities let Hagar and Pogo go the next morning. I guess the police thought they were harmless enough. But as far as they knew, Rothschild was still in custody. No one at the house had heard from him since he was taken in, and no one could get a hold of his family for an update.

"He was the brains of the project," Pogo said.

Hagar added, "He was the one with all the connections."

They were quite a pair, the two of them. At one point, they paused the conversation to repack their bong with some more opium-infused weed. Then when they finished, they passed it to Daniel, who graciously partook of the smoke, while they proceeded to finish their story.

I suppose the first shocking thing they told us was that the story we read in the paper about them planning to drop Edwin's coffin on Paul Revere's doorsteps was all a lie, a fiction concocted by the chief of police, or the cemetery, or someone else. They had no idea.

"It's total bullshit," Pogo said. "We wanted to dig up his grave. That part's true, but not so we could snatch the coffin. We wanted to cut a sample so we could do the test ourselves. We had a forensic scientist in Charlestown all lined up to do it. It would have been the greatest hack of all time."

"What do you mean, you wanted to do the test?" asked Daniel, flummoxed. "How did you plan on getting a hold of the museum's sample?"

This is where things really got bizarre.

According to Hagar and Pogo, Rothschild had been planning to dig up Edwin's grave ever since he arrived at MIT as a freshman. They got involved only about a year ago, they said, after Rothschild, now a senior, showed them a computer program he had developed that was able to calculate the probability John Wilkes Booth escaped from the barn, weighing all available evidence.

"I was blown away by it," Hagar said. "The formula was flawless."

Apparently, Rothschild had been studying the Booth escape theory since he was in middle school. An eccentric uncle turned him onto the idea and helped him collect and sort much of the evidence and materials he would eventually use in constructing the elaborate algorithm that ultimately convinced Hagar and Pogo to go along with his plan.

"Weighing every piece of evidence you can imagine evenly," Pogo said, "it calculated the chance Booth got away to be 81.603 per cent certain."

"You're fucking kidding me," Daniel said, in complete disbelief.

"That's what I thought the first time he showed it to me," said Pogo, "but after I looked at the code, I couldn't argue with the result."

"Of course, that still means there's an eighteen per cent chance they got him," Hagar added. "That's a pretty significant figure, too."

"Sure it is," Daniel said, "but whatever the figure is, it still doesn't add up to a testable sample of the man in the barn. How were you going to get a hold of that? Were you going to break into the Army Medical Museum too?"

They both laughed.

"No," Hagar said, "we were going to test the mummy."

In an instant, my whole body went numb. Daniel nearly jumped out of his skin.

He blurted out, "What do you mean? You have the mummy?" meaning the corpse of "David E. George" that Finis L. Bates had preserved at the morgue in Enid back in 1903.

It was impossible. No one knew where the mummy was. How could these clowns have it? It was last seen in New Hope, Pennsylvania in 1976. Nate had spent a lifetime looking for it without success. The possessor of the mummy, potentially, held all the answers. In 1930 a group of six medical physicians in Chicago performed a thorough autopsy on the mummy and concluded it had to be John Wilkes Booth. It was the exact same height and age the assassin would have been, and it had all the peculiar markings and irregularities the assassin had in life, the scar on the back of its neck from Dr. May's surgery, a deformed thumb, the arched right eyebrow, and a thickened fibula, apart from the fact that it looked exactly like John Wilkes Booth.

Hagar and Pogo looked like nice enough kids. They seemed to me to be honest. Much of their story up until this point had been convincing. It was hard to imagine what they might gain by making any of it up. But how could it be possible? I thought to myself, could it be true? Of all the people on the planet, Hagar and Pogo had actually found the mummy?

It turned out neither Hagar, nor Pogo, nor Rothschild, as far as they knew, actually had the mummy in their possession. It was Rothschild's uncle, the same uncle who introduced him to the Booths in the first place, they said, who supposedly had access to the mummy and had arranged for it to be tested. Evidently, he had a very unusual connection in the secretive underground world of human cadaver trafficking, a very dangerous business, first of all, because it's illegal to own a cadaver in the United States today, but second, and more dangerously, because of all the harmful chemicals handlers of cadavers are exposed to on a consistent basis. Prolonged exposure has terrible effects on your health.

"Just think about what could have happened if you actually succeeded," Daniel told them.

He was exploding out of his skin. He kept asking them a hundred different ways if they knew how he might be able to get in touch with Rothschild's uncle about the mummy. And over and over and over again they kept telling him they were sorry, but they couldn't help. Rothschild was the only person who had the info, they said. Thankfully, Daniel had sense enough not to ask them if he could go poking around his room, not that he would have found anything anyway. I remember hearing them say at some point in our conversation that Rothschild, who was a master programmer, never trusted anyone, as a result, anything he may have been working on would have been mightily encrypted.

Finally, over the course of several hours, which included a gigantic Indian dinner downstairs with the rest of the fraternity, and bushels of marijuana and beer, he finally chilled out. After dinner, Hagar and Pogo and Knave took us up to the rooftop of the house, where we drank and smoked the night away with several other fraternity members in the glow of the Boston skyline.

It was a perfect night. The sky was clear and the temperature was quite balmy. We could see the full moon in all its glory. When we stepped out on the roof deck, we all commented on its beauty and discussed the significance of the earlier eclipse, before moving on to an epic discussion about the rest of the galaxy and molecular nanotechnology machines the size of refrigerators that can turn moonshine into apples, and about a thousand other transgressions, including a pointed dissertation by Knave about the profound significance of the number twenty-two in our universe.

I guess I was having such a good time, somewhere along the course of the night, I ordered two kegs of beer to be delivered to the house. I have no recollection of placing the order, but I vaguely recall several fraternity brothers toasting me after carrying the kegs to the roof. Apparently I didn't want the night to end. I think I even participated in a tai chi session one of the guys was leading at one point, which is something I had never done before. It was a mind-altering experience that, among other things, completely tuned out all of the Booth hysteria that had been developing as recently as our visit to Hagar and Pogo's fun house, just hours before.

Intoxicated by all the festivities and camaraderie, I forgot all about John and the mummy. There were so many other more important ideas, like nanotechnology and new uses for the space station, buzzing around the roof that night, I couldn't give a damn about the Booths. They were expelled from my body with each puff of pot I exhaled and piss I took, until, that is, the sun was shining in my face the next morning. Then, without fail, the Booths promptly returned to me. I was woken by the sound of their voice.

"Shit," Daniel said with alarm. "It's already seven. I've got to get back to the cemetery for the interment," and suddenly it became evident to me that we had so much fun the night before, we ended up spending the night on the roof.

I looked around for Hagar and Pogo, but they were nowhere to be found, nor was any other life form, aside from us, unless you count the yeast in the beer kegs and the half-filled cups that lined the roof. Apart from that, all the Chi was gone, which struck me in a profound way.

I truly felt transformed by the night in a way that's hard to describe. It was very different from any of the many benders of my past. As the moon orbited along its ellipse that night, a deep stirring occurred in my brain, unlike anything I had experienced in a long, long time. The eloquence of thought and open mindedness of such a college of capable young thinkers, so passionately committed to solving a broad array of problems I had never even considered before, was infectious. As I stood on the roof of the Parthenon that dawn, squinting at the sober sun, I sincerely questioned whether it was all just an opium-inspired illusion, Hagar and Pogo? The Booth algorithm? The mummy? The number twenty-two? Or was I truly changed forever?

THE CASTLE

When I got back to New York it didn't take long for me to settle down into my normal routine of pool and scotch. I tried my best to drown all thoughts of the test from my mind. What good would it do to dwell on the inevitable, I reasoned, but it was difficult. Speculation about the pending results was all anyone around the club could talk about. I was surprised, myself, by how much emotional capital I suddenly had invested in the outcome. For someone who began as an impartial observer, I was amazed by how much my thinking on the matter had evolved. It was an astonishing reversal, one I never predicted.

Daniel, on the other hand, was off on an entirely different trajectory all together. While I was trying my damnedest at the Players to escape thoughts of Booth, he was burning alive in the barn. The mummy was out there within reach and, before everything was over, he was determined to find it. When not at his desk at The Beacon, he spent every other waking moment trying to track down Rothschild and his uncle and every other lead imaginable in pursuit of that mummy, but nothing ever materialized. It was a frustrating time for him because, up until this point, he had gotten just about everything he ever wanted for his story, but the mummy was too hard to get. Finally, thirty-odd days after the exhumation of Edwin, the development he was waiting for came along to take his mind off it.

Daniel, along with everybody else, received the email from the Smithsonian inviting us to attend the press conference at Institution headquarters in Washington, also known as "The Castle," where, "at long last, the answer to this age-old mystery will be revealed."

The day of reckoning ultimately fell on the Friday after Memorial Day. I arrived in Washington late the night before and checked in to the Hay-Adams again, only this time I was by myself. I don't know when Daniel got in, or where he stayed, or ate, or anything else he did in the days leading up to the announcement. We had very little contact ever since we returned from Cambridge. In fact, until that day at the Castle, I hadn't seen him in weeks. I only knew about his hunt for the mummy via the occasional text or line of email, and by what he relayed to me that afternoon in the pressroom.

On the day of the big event, it didn't take me long to get to the Castle, or rather outside of it. I stepped out of the hotel and walked across the Mall between the Washington Monument and the Capitol. The conditions couldn't have been more perfect. The wind was calm, the temperature was seventy-two, and the sky looked like a reflection of the Smithsonian coat of arms, a flaming orange sun at the center of a brilliant indigo disc. But from the moment I stepped up to the main gate to when I actually stepped foot inside the press room felt like a dark eternity.

The security was torture. They had one old guard meticulously combing through every bag, purse, and coat, and each cameraman must have lugged ten bags, it seemed. Thankfully, once I got into the press room things thinned out a bit. Only appropriately credentialed personnel were permitted to enter this area. Everyone else had to set up shop in the halls.

Inside, I saw Lois straight away. She was sitting next to Nate in the front row of the auditorium. Behind them, there was an audience of anywhere from seventy to a hundred people raked upwards in rows to the highest point in the room where all the video cameras were stationed, their lenses aimed at a modest-sized stage below that soon enough would be the final platform for the Booths.

I looked around and saw pretty much everyone who mattered in attendance, except for Peggy. Daniel told me, she purposely busied herself on the farm because she was too nervous to witness the whole thing live, but would definitely be watching it all on television. This story was later corroborated by Peggy.

Another noticeable absence was Richard Chandler. I kept waiting for the old man to show up and bare his grisly teeth, but he never came. Although, knowing what I know today, he was likely watching everything remotely from some undisclosed underground location.

But looking back, I have to say the absence that I can't believe didn't arouse more suspicion at the time was that of Peter Ramsey. For a man of his stature to go so seamlessly undetected on such a big occasion is truly a marvel of deception. No one even mentioned his name. Then again, there was a lot going on to distract even the sharpest of minds.

While everyone waited for the show to begin, reporters and producers, left and right, left no grave un-dug lining up interviews, before and after, with anyone in the room who would talk to them about the results, and Daniel was certainly among them. He was right in the thick of it.

Back and forth he darted around the room, talking to this person one minute and that person the next. He was firing on all cylinders. His facial expressions and mannerisms were very animated, even more so than usual. Another notable aspect of his appearance that struck me at the time was his hair. For whatever reason, he had altered it for the occasion. Instead of his usual slicked-back-straight hairstyle, it was extremely short on the sides of his head with the long strands on top parted dramatically over one side of his forehead, like a fancy poodle roll, or like some royal magistrate. It was a radically different look for him and took a while for me to get accustomed to it, in which time the ceremony finally got underway.

According to my watch, it was a minute past two when Wayne Clough, the Secretary General of the Smithsonian Institution, walked onstage in a suit and tie and took the emblem-crested podium that was the centerpiece of the press conference. In the background, Dr. Kay and Dr. Foley filed in in their lab coats, along with a phalanx of forensic researchers that lined up behind them. Their entrance triggered a flurry of excitement in the room. The clicking and snapping of cameras was incessant.

As soon as everyone was in place, Secretary Clough got down to business, first by welcoming everyone and thanking us all for coming, then by launching into a passionate speech about the value of scientific inquiry in society and its profound impact on human civilization. He told us that we were all extremely lucky to be living at a time of such unprecedented scientific advancement, and that one of the most central arteries of that advancement was undoubtedly the exponential progress we have made in our understanding of DNA.

The secretary reminded us that while much of our attention concerning DNA, quite justly, has been turned to the criminal system and profiling, its development over the last twenty years has only just begun to solve some of the most vexing riddles known to man.

Indeed, up until that afternoon the most famous DNA identification in history centered on the most romantic legend of the Russian Revolution, that Grand Duchess Anastasia, the youngest daughter of Czar Nicholas II, and her brother Alexei escaped the fate of the rest of their family, who in 1918 were gunned-down by Red Guard officers under the command of Vladimir Lenin. Similar to John Wilkes Booth, the legend of their survival spread almost instantly.

By the early twenties, Anna Anderson had come forward and insisted that she was Anastasia, and by the end of the nineties, Disney made an animated film inspired by the story. By that time, the escape theory gained traction after DNA tests confirmed that two Romanov bodies, a boy and a girl, were, in fact, missing from the family's mass grave in Yekaterinburg, Russia. But when another, smaller grave nearby was discovered years later containing a pile of burnt and broken bones, a century's worth of speculation came to a grinding halt. Archeologists were convinced they were the remains of the missing Romanov children and in 2009 proved it. Through genetic analysis of mitochondrial DNA and the nuclear genome, both the autosomes and the Y-chromosomes, they confirmed the familial relationships and laid to rest one of the most enduring legends of all time.

"Scientific experiments of this sort," the secretary said in closing, "may one day reveal to us the great secrets of our universe. This is why the Smithsonian Institution is so pleased to be a part of the historic announcement we have for you today." And with that, he introduced and surrendered the podium to Dr. Kay.

Not coincidentally, sitting in the audience observing all of this was the man ultimately responsible for the Romanov identification, as well as the Booth identification that was about to unfold before us, the father of DNA fingerprinting himself, Dr. Alec Jeffreys. Before the event began, Daniel had an opportunity to interview him. I happened to be standing nearby when Daniel asked him what he thought about being passed up for the Nobel Prize, yet again. I couldn't help but eavesdrop on his answer. Sir Jeffreys chuckled at the question. Evidently, the Queen of England found his achievements commendable enough.

"Well," he answered in perfect Oxford English, with almost as much color as his red trousers. "Who am I to argue with the Nobel committee? They're a smart bunch," and chuckled again.

Daniel followed up the quip by pointing out that the last time the Prize was awarded for anything DNA related was back in 1962 for the discovery of the double helix. "Isn't it about time they awarded another one?" he said.

Sir Jeffreys nodded and chuckled again and responded by saying, "Seriously, there are a lot of talented people out there making incredible advancements. Most scientists don't get into our line of work to win prizes. At the end of the day, I'm thankful that I've been able to make any contribution at all. The fields of science and medicine are expanding now at such a rapid rate."

These were certainly modest words from a true genius. Though I suppose, at this point, Sir Jeffreys would be a better candidate for the Peace Prize, rather than that for science, given his incalculable contributions to civilized society, not only now, but for innumerable generations to come. Any who dispute this should speak to my friend Peter Neufeld, the co-founder of The Innocence Project, which has exonerated hundreds of falsely convicted prisoners in the U.S. since its founding in 1992, several of whom were on death-row, all through DNA profiling.

Another memorable moment that sticks out in my mind before the feature event began occurred during another interview with Nate Orlowek. I was sitting right next to him at the time, but this time it wasn't Daniel conducting the interview. It was some reporter, a woman, I didn't know or recognize and never saw again. All I can say is that it was a privilege to listen to their conversation.

After asking Nate all the usual questions about Booth and David E. George and John St. Helen and so on that he had answered a thousand times before, the young reporter asked a rather pointed question that, I could tell, really impressed him.

"For forty years you've been pushing to make this day happen," she said. "Now that it's here, how do you feel, knowing that this man who you've helped sensationalize in the process, is ultimately a very bad person? More evil perhaps than Osama Bin Laden?"

Nate smiled and nodded his head at the question for a few moments before answering. In characteristic fashion, he wanted to be very precise with his response.

"Have you ever seen the movie Field of Dreams?" he asked her.

The reporter blinked before answering coldly, "Sure, I've seen it," as if to say, what's the f-ing point? But Nate just smiled again.

"I love that movie," he said, "in part because I have a soft spot for baseball. My uncle was the first Jewish baseball player ever to play in a Major League Baseball All-Star game."

This little tidbit perked the young reporter up. She jotted the factoid down in her pad, while Nate continued.

"But what I really love about that film, I mean truly love, is that it has absolutely nothing to do with baseball. Now people say to me all the time, 'Nate, what do you mean it has nothing to do with baseball? It's a film about baseball.' It has absolutely nothing at all to do with baseball. This is how I feel about John Wilkes Booth.

"At this point, John Wilkes Booth has absolutely nothing to do with John Wilkes Booth for me. This whole journey, or expedition, as they're calling it now, has really all along been about," and he paused for a noticeable moment before saying, "my dad.

"To me, Booth is really nothing more than an abstraction, a cartoon I almost in no way associate with Lincoln's assassin. I mean, that part of history is done and settled. All John Wilkes Booth means to me now is finality, about committing to a project and seeing it through to the end. That's, in many ways, the enduring lesson of my father, who instilled in me this discipline. When, as a teenager, I discovered that history as it is written might not be correct, he said to me, 'So what are you gonna do about it?' And when later I began to waver in my commitment to it, he reminded me of the value of perseverance and the enlightenment that comes from sticking to a long-term goal. If right now they announce Booth did it, he got away, or if Dr. Kay says he was killed at the barn," and he paused again here for a thoughtful moment, "it won't make any difference to me. At this point, I've done my part. I've achieved my goal. And frankly, now I'm free."

These were the words cycling around my brain as Dr. Kay took to the podium and briefed the press, telling them step by step about the process she and the team went through to determine their result. How first they bleached the samples to get rid of any contaminants, then how they washed them again with regular soap and water to remove any residue that may have remained from the bleach. And how after that, the samples were exposed to UV light and after that, ground into a fine powder, before actually beginning the extraction process, which took days of exposing the bone powder to a barrage of chemicals to separate the DNA, like iron from ore, and the other various steps required to break down the various organic and inorganic components to release the DNA. Then, once everyone-in-the-room's heads were spinning, she began describing the sequencing process, and the difference between mitochondrial DNA, which follows the maternal lineage and does not participate in the process of genetic recombination, and nuclear DNA, which houses the Y-chromosome, passed down virtually unchanged from father to son, and the number of molecular photocopies the team took of both varieties using the technique of short tandem repeats, "STRs," and the number of test tubes that were run through the capillaries of large machines that were read by lasers and amplified, and sequenced, and compared to the corresponding sequences of the man shot in the barn.

"After following all these steps, with the full support of the staff you see behind me, who have worked tirelessly around the clock for the past month and a half, Dr. Foley and I have concluded, independently, with the highest degree of certainty available to us today that John Wilkes Booth," and here she paused to nudge her glasses up ever so slightly from the bridge of her nose, at which point, out of nowhere, Daniel abruptly stood up and rushed out of the room before the announcement was made. Luckily, he was standing close enough to the door, so that his exit didn't create too much of a distraction, but I certainly noticed it. What was he thinking? I thought.

And then Dr. Kay put an end to all the anticipation.

"Today we can say with certainty that John Wilkes Booth perished in the barn on April 26th, 1865."

Just like that, it was over. The official verdict was in, and Daniel wasn't even in the room to hear it.

THE CALL

The room exploded as a hundred reporters raised their voices and hands to demand a thousand follow-up answers from the good doctor.

Strangely, after all these years, I had no detectible reaction. I couldn't sense a thing inside. It was as if Dr. Kay had spoken Greek. Finally, the riddle had been revealed, and it didn't seem to matter at all. Nothing had changed.

I looked around the room at Nate and Lois and the others and they all had the same expressions on their faces. It wasn't anguish. It wasn't surprise. It wasn't disappointment. It wasn't anything. Perhaps it was shock, but I don't think so. It was a revelation, an epiphany that confirms the great and powerful universal language of the ages. They got it right after all. There was no disputing it now. The whole thing was settled, once and for all. It should have been a reaffirming boost of confidence in mankind, but somehow it wasn't.

As the press swarmed, "the expedition" team just sat there demoralized in their seats, motionless, as it began to sink in. They knew what was ahead, all the answers they were obliged to provide now to the throngs of reporters and photographers that lined the halls of the Castle eagerly awaiting their comments. To their satisfaction, Nate and Lois didn't keep them waiting very long. They were good sports about the whole thing. They left the pressroom minutes after Dr. Kay made the announcement and stoically stood in front of the cameras while the media threw eggs at them.

I was the only member of our team to stay in the pressroom afterwards. I waited for Daniel to return. While all the other reporters fought like wolves to tear into Dr. Kay behind the podium, I just sat there expecting him to walk through the door any minute and wrestle control of the room. Maybe he had to go to the bathroom, I thought, or maybe he just needed some fresh air. But after witnessing a solid grilling of Dr. Kay for a good ten minutes, finally I couldn't take it anymore and decided to leave the inquisition behind.

The minute I stepped out of the pressroom, microphones and flashes were in my face. Thankfully, once they discovered I was a nobody, they kindly let me be. They were only interested in the big fish. As I searched for Daniel down the great corridor, I saw Lois talking to CBS News on one side of the hall and Nate talking to FOX on the other. Then a little further down, I saw Kathy entertaining a gaggle of reporters next to some priceless statue of a Smithsonian president. I saw Michael. I even saw Anderson Cooper, but no Daniel.

When I walked past Anderson I couldn't help but overhear him say over his CNN microphone, "Well, at bedtime tonight, as countless parents are asked to explain to their children what happened to President Lincoln's killer, they won't have to lie. The story we've been telling for a hundred and fifty years is true. We got the bad guy."

A comforting story, indeed, I thought, and in a few more paces I was out the door. I looked around outside the Castle, but Daniel was nowhere to be seen. What the fuck, I thought to myself.

For a second I considered going back in to see if somehow I overlooked him, but then I came to my senses. "Fuck it," I said, "I'm not going back in there." It was like losing the World Series. Who wants to stick around at the stadium? Besides, I thought for sure Daniel would get in touch with me sooner or later after he calmed down and he'd explain everything over a drink or ten back at the hotel. All afternoon I waited for him at the bar. I drank myself into oblivion, but he never came. Not a call. Not a text.

I have no idea how I got to my room that night, but somehow or other I made it, because when my phone rang at two in the morning, I was safe and sound in my bed. At first I ignored it and it stopped. But when it rang again, it began to dawn on me through my inebriated dreams that it might be Daniel calling about something important and so I roused myself and answered the call, but to my surprise when I picked up, it wasn't Daniel. It was Peggy. The trembling in her voice moved me in a way I can't describe.

"The police just called," she said. "Daniel's been in an accident."

For a second I thought I was dreaming. I couldn't process what she was telling me.

"I'm taking the first train I can get," she continued, "but that won't get in until morning. You're the only person I know to contact.

Is there any way you can go to the police station and get more information?"

"Of course," I said, still half-asleep, and asked her what else the police told her.

"They just told me it was an automobile accident and that it was very serious. My name came up on the computer, because the car's registered in my name."

I told her to relax and take a deep breath and promised her I would head over to the station right away and find out what happened and pick her up at the train station when she got in.

"Thank you Al," she said. She most definitely was in tears.

As soon as I hung up the phone, I raced over to the precinct that contacted her. It was still the dead of night when I got there about a half-hour later. There couldn't have been more than a dozen cops on duty, all milling around like zombies. I walked up to the first one who made eye contact with me and told him who I was and asked if he could give me the details.

According to the official police report, Daniel's, or rather Peggy's, car went careening off Rock Creek Parkway, just below the Watergate Hotel, and flipped into the Potomac River by the Roosevelt bridge, just up river from the Lincoln monument. The incident occurred at approximately 10:05 pm.

When I asked the officer if Daniel was dead or alive, I was alarmed when he told me they hadn't found a body yet. After they pulled the car out of the water and discovered there was no one in the car, a team was dispatched to search for any survivors, but couldn't find anyone. The officer told me a more expansive effort would resume in the morning that would hopefully be more successful, but nothing more could effectively be done that night.

After the officer told me all this, I stuck around the station for a few more minutes and tried to process all the information. This was certainly not anything I expected to hear. When it finally clicked in my brain that practically nothing more could be done until morning, I slowly walked out of the station and drove back to the hotel in a trance-like state.

When I got back to my room, I couldn't sleep. I didn't know what to do with myself. Surprisingly, for the first time in I can't remember how long, the last thing I wanted was a drink. I paced the room restlessly, not knowing what to do next. I turned the television on and then just as quickly turned it off. I couldn't concentrate. Then something caught my eye across the room. It was my phone. It was blinking where I left it when I returned to the room.

I'm not one of these junkies who checks his phone every second. I frequently go long stretches without looking at the thing and purposefully leave it out of reach for this reason, but on this particular occasion, the flash was irresistible.

I picked it up and was instantly shocked. At the top of the screen was an email from "David E. George." The subject line read, "Via con Dios."

22

THE EMAIL

My heart pounded as I opened the message.

"Doc," it read, "you're the only person I can trust."

It was unmistakably Daniel's writing, but unlike his usual correspondence and previous notes that were always impeccably, if not overly, punctuated, this email barely contained a single comma. He was obviously in a rush when he composed it.

I'm sending you this now from a phantom email account in hopes no one can track it or if they can it takes a long time. Just before they announced the result in the press room I got a text from Hagar out of the blue telling me he was with Rothschild and that they had just located the mummy but it was about to be destroyed unless I could find a way to stop it. He told me where I had to go and told me they were on their way too but that I was closer. John got away, Doc. We were betrayed.

Attached is the audio recording of what went down what I could get of it anyway. Peter Francesca Chandler.....they

were all in on it. ITs all in the recording!.................. Promise
me that if anything happens to me, you'll make sure this gets
out……….................

PS: Also take care of mom. Don't let her get dragged into
this.

Via con Dios,
D. E. G.

I immediately opened the file and started listening. Below is a transcription of the recording. My apologies if at times it's a bit shady. I was able to make out most of the spoken words, but as for the background details, I have only a vague picture of who was actually at the meeting, how they got there, and what exactly took place. I have virtually no point of reference, other than what the voices told me, and what little I could deduce from the few distant and scratchy ambient clues I was able to pull from the recording.

All of this withstanding, from the beginning of this chronicle until now, I urge you to consider this following piece of evidence and draw from it your final conclusion on this matter of John Wilkes Booth. Take from it what you will and act as you must. It is yours.

23

THE TRANSCRIPT

Friday, May 31, 9:30 P.M.

RECORDING BEGINS with what sounds like gears churning.

DANIEL: What are you doing here? Are you in on this?

A voice that sounds like Peter Ramsey responds.

PETER: You shouldn't have come here, Daniel.

DANIEL: Who is that? Is that Chandler?

PETER: Hey, you can't go over there.

Fumbling and popping of the audio muffles the sound of movement.

A voice that sounds like Dick Chandler pipes in.

CHANDLER: Let him in. He can't do anything now.

More fumbling and popping drowns out movement. Then the audio cuts in and out, and when it cuts in again Chandler's voice sounds closer and more intimate.

CHANDLER (CONT.): Are you afraid?

DANIEL: Why should I be afraid?

Pause.

CHANDLER: You're in a strange place.

DANIEL: Is that the mummy?

Pause.

CHANDLER: Would you like to see for yourself?

DANIEL: I would.

CHANDLER: Help him Peter.

Silence, followed by an audible gasp.

CHANDLER (CONT.): Why so pale, Daniel? Isn't this why you came here?

Brief silence.

DANIEL: Where did you find this?

CHANDLER: I am the swallow. I am the scorpion. I am the snake whose years are long. I am the fishes of Horus, great one in the Bitter Lakes.

DANIEL: Is it really him?

Pause.

CHANDLER: Of course it's him. Don't you trust your own reporting? How else did you think we were able to produce the result?

DANIEL: So Booth actually got away.

CHANDLER: *I wouldn't say that…. But it's true.*

Brief pause.

DANIEL: *And am I a Booth?*

Pause.

CHANDLER: *At this point, who the fuck cares? No, you're not. Are you happy? At this point, what difference does it make…?*

DANIEL: *You can't destroy this mummy.*

CHANDLER: *Alas, I'm afraid we must. This task is long overdue.*

DANIEL: *I'll blow the whole fucking whistle on it.*

CHANDLER: *No, Mr. Boland, I'm afraid you will not.*

Pause.

DANIEL: *Why? Who's going to stop me? Peter? Tell me. Who's going to stop me?*

CHANDLER: *Mr. Boland, you are going to stop yourself.*

DANIEL: *What the fuck are you talking about?*

CHANDLER: *Daniel, Daniel, Daniel. We've been profiling you for a long, long time. Our file on you is this thick. Tell him Peter.*

PETER: *It's thick.*

CHANDLER: *Did you actually think you could blow the top off all of this and get away with it, Mr. Boland? What about Joan Stevens? What did that poor woman do to deserve your wrath? You brutally murdered that woman.*

Silence.

CHANDLER (CONT.): Answer me!

Pause.

DANIEL: That's bullshit and you know it.

CHANDLER: Is it really now? This man has the proof, her truck with your fingerprints all over it.

Silence.

DANIEL: You did this.

CHANDLER: Who's going to believe you?

Long silence.

CHANDLER (CONT.): I know it must be painful. A tragedy, really, that it has to be like this. But you left us no other choice. There's just too much at stake. But not to worry. We'll let you live. Go back to your little cubicle at the paper. You're no threat to us anymore. You can leave here and resume your life like normal, like nothing ever happened. We don't hold any of this against you. In fact, you have a bright future ahead of you, should you choose it. A person with your skills could be a congressman or a senator.

Silence.

Sound of muffled movement.

CHANDLER (CONT.): You have no other choice Daniel Boland!

Sound of more muffled movement.

END of RECORDING.

. . .

It's a lot to swallow, I know. It also must be stated that the voice on the audio recording has yet to be positively verified as that of Richard Chandler's, but a copy of the recording is available for this purpose at a moment's notice, upon request. It calls into question everything. Did Chandler really obtain the mummy? Did he somehow manage to swap a sample from the mummy for the specimens believed to be John Wilkes Booth's? Was David E. George truly John Wilkes Booth? I confess, the prospect is extremely disturbing. It's driven me to near madness. Has it all been one big conspiracy after all?

THE IDENTIFICATION

A few hours later I picked up Peggy at Union Station. As soon as she stepped into the car, I told her about Daniel's email and the recording and what the police officer had just told me. I said it was best to brace herself for the worst, but I had no idea what we might discover. That's when she broke down in tears.

When Peggy finally calmed down enough to speak, she told me all about her relationship with Daniel's father, John William Boland, "but we all called him Jack."

They had known each other since they were small children. Their parents were close friends. For as far back as Peggy could remember, her father and Jack's father used to ride and go shooting together, "and while the men were out carousing, my mom and Jack's mom would knit and gab and cook for us kids."

Peggy was a year older than Jack. She said he always worshipped the ground she walked on, but as a young girl, the age gap made it impossible for her to think of him as anything other than a surrogate younger brother. All of this changed, however, after they both graduated from high school. Being young and single in rural Pennsylvania didn't suit either one of them for very long. Soon enough, they were riding together on the sprawling grounds of the Wood family compound and, before Peggy knew it, she was pregnant with Daniel. The rest is history.

Daniel was two years old when Jack died in a car crash. "It was a terrible accident," Peggy told me. "It sent Jane, Jack's mother, into a horrible depression." This depression was compounded less than six months later when Jack's father died suddenly from unknown causes. "After Hank's death, Jane withdrew from the world. She pretty much refused to see anybody, except me and my mother. She became quite paranoid and, increasingly, began to blame herself for Jack's death."

Thankfully, Jane's suffering didn't last long. She passed away less than a year after her husband's death. In that time, however, she shared many strange stories with Peggy, along with breathtaking evidence linking the family to the Booths, that Peggy was reluctant to believe, until now.

It was incredible to hear her talk this way. I couldn't help but think is this what Mary Ann went through with Edwin when they were called upon to identify the remains of John? Could all of this really be true?

When we walked through the main door of the police station, it seemed like everyone in the place was waiting for us. Since my visit, less than six hours before, the search team had found a body floating down by the Navy Yard, a home run away from Nationals Park. They asked if we would identify it. Peggy and I both agreed and a few minutes later an officer appeared to escort us into the morgue.

The body was laid out for us on a stainless steel table when we walked into the room, just like Edwin was in Cambridge, only with a white sheet cloaking it. But just before the medical examiner was about to de-cloak the corpse for us, Peggy suddenly panicked.

"I'm not sure I can go through with this," she said, and turned toward me for cover. She was terrified by what she might see.

I surprised myself by being supportive. I hugged her and she accepted it, which felt unexpectedly good.

"We have to," I told her. "Daniel's either alive or dead, and it's our responsibility to confirm it either way."

Peggy didn't need my words of wisdom, but perhaps in this unusual moment, she was comforted by the human touch.

A few seconds later, the examiner pulled down the sheet and showed us the body. Lying naked on the table before us, it was clear the corpse looked nothing like Daniel. The cut and color of his hair was a shade off, and his teeth, and complexion, and overall appearance were greatly altered. The body was roughly the same height and build as Daniel, but apart from that, there were too many inconsistencies to be convincing. But if this man wasn't Daniel, who else could he be? How in this day and age could anyone stage a false death? Who else would have to be in on it? Where would they get the body? How could it not be Daniel?

In absolute silence Peggy and I took our time carefully examining the body. As we did this I thought about Daniel's last wish, via con Dios, and imagined that that afternoon I dropped him off at the Mexican Embassy for his Beacon story, maybe, just maybe, in that brief window he was able to offer them something of value in exchange for asylum, that while we were examining this corpse, he was in Mexico City, or maybe even Havana by now, alive and well, far from Chandler's reach. But who would have stuck their neck out for Daniel? What could he have possibly offered them?

No, I resolved in the immediate moment following our examination, that that corpse was unquestionably Daniel. Then shortly afterwards, when the time was right, Peggy looked at me square in the eyes, and then the crypt keeper, and said, "That's him. That's my son, Daniel Boland. The birthmark just below his right elbow confirms it completely."

What other option was there? What good could come from any other outcome? In that moment, as painful as it was for both of us to admit, Daniel was better off dead than alive. I can only hope that a more fortunate path lies ahead for him in the afterlife, if such a place exists. Yes, it hurts me deeply to say it, but this is my final word on the subject. I hereby swear, in the name of the father, the son, and the un-holy Booth, everything I have written herein is the truth.

Yours truly,

Dr. Alfred Fredrick Pearson

ACKNOWLEDGMENTS

So many people helped make this book possible. I hardly know where to begin. I suppose I never would have known anything about the proposal to exhume Edwin Booth were it not for my old friend, Al Pearson, who graciously gave me permission to use his name fictitiously as the narrator of this story.

Then of course there is Nate Orlowek, the ringleader of the real escape research team. He granted me unrestricted access to his decades' worth of research, put me in touch with so many others who made this book possible, and always made himself available to me whenever I had any questions. He is a smart, thoughtful, and caring person. Without his help and trust none of this could have been possible. I am honored to call him a friend and thank him, as well, for agreeing to be a fictional character in this book.

Next in line I must thank Edwin's great-great granddaughter, Lois Trebisacci. Her assistance and friendship throughout was an inspiration and I shall never forget it. While on the subject of Booth descendants, I must also thank Joanne Hulme and John T. Booth, two very thoughtful and opened minded human beings. All three of these people represent the best of the Booth family. I hope they never give up their drive to discover the truth about their heritage.

Then there's Stuart Miller. The debt I owe him for patiently mentoring me all these years will not be paid in full soon. He is a true friend, fabulous writer, and exceptional teacher. He helped me from the very start of the process and edited nearly every draft to the end. Thank you, Stuart. I won't forget it.

I also need to thank Sarah Smith and David Black for reading and giving me feedback on my early drafts, as well as, Nathan Rostron, who helped me in the later stages.

From a research standpoint, this book would have been a very hollow read were it not for Mark Zaid, Francis Gorman, Dr. Krista Latham (Assistant Professor of Biology & Anthropology at University of Indianapolis Molecular Anthropology Laboratory), Ken Taylor (Vice-President of Operations at Green-Wood Cemetery), Michael Kauffman (author of "American Brutus"), The Surratt Society, in particular, Laurie Verge and Joan Chaconas, and Scott Taylor (Lauinger Library at Georgetown University Special Collections Research Center). Each was instrumental in providing me with the materials I needed to write this story. Thank you all very much.

The best way I know how to express my gratitude to the pioneers and true historians of this subject is to list the names of those who were most influential to me and recommend you read their books. What more could an author want?

Find out more for yourself about: Otto Eisenschiml (Why Was Lincoln Murdered?), Finis L. Bates (The Escape and Suicide of John

Wilkes Booth), Leonard Guttridge and Ray Neff (Dark Union), C. Wyatt Evans (The Legend of John Wilkes Booth), Theodore Roscoe (The Web of Conspiracy), Nora Titone (My Thoughts Be Bloody), James Swanson (Manhunt), Doris Kearns Goodwin (Team of Rivals), Bill O'Reilly (Killing Lincoln), and the exhaustive papers of James O. Hall, W. P. Campbell, and Dr. Clarence Wilson.

And of course I would be terribly remiss if I didn't thank my ever-patient and tolerant wife, the beautiful Jennifer Parsons. I know it's not easy being married to a writer. I appreciate everything you do for our family.

Last, but certainly not least, I must acknowledge the members and staff of The Players, who were more or less the inspiration for this book. If you told me this is where my membership would take me when I joined the club over a decade ago, I never would have believed you.

www.ingramcontent.com/pod-product-compliance
Lightning Source LLC
Chambersburg PA
CBHW022130050726
47590CB00002B/492